Lapham Rising

Rising

Lapham

A NOVEL

ROGER ROSENBLATT

+/06

HarperCollins books may be purchased for educational, business, or sales promotional use. For information, please write: Special Markets Department, HarperCollins Publishers, 10 East 53rd Street, New York, NY 10022.

Designed by Jessica Shatan Heslin

Library of Congress Cataloging-in-Publication Data

Rosenblatt, Roger.
    Lapham rising / Roger Rosenblatt.—1st Ecco ed.
      p. cm.
    ISBN-10: 0-06-083361-0
    ISBN-13: 978-0-06-083361-9
    1. Hamptons (N.Y.)—Fiction. I. Title.

    PS3618.O335L37 2006
    813'.54—dc22   2005048835

06 07 08 09 10 WBC/RRD 10 9 8 7 6 5 4 3 2

"There!" Lapham pounded with his great, hairy fist on the envelope he had been addressing. "William!" he called out, and he handed the letter to a boy who came to get it. "I want that to go right away. Well, sir," he continued, wheeling round in his leather-cushioned swivel-chair, and facing Bartley, seated so near that their knees almost touched, "so you want my life, death, and Christian sufferings, do you, young man?"

"That's what I'm after," said Bartley. "Your money or your life."

"I guess you wouldn't want my life without the money," said Lapham.

William Dean Howells, *The Rise of Silas Lapham*

Lapham Rising

Bang bang bang bang bang. I start to flip out of bed, forgetting that Hector is beside me. I roll over on top of him. He bites my ear. I attempt to bite his. Another perfect summer day begins in the Hamptons.

"Goddammit it, Hector!" I slap on a bandage, grab my clothes, and head outside.

"Taketh not the Lord's name in vain," he says, then flattens himself, tail and all, and returns to sleep. Nothing on earth is snootier than a West Highland white terrier, especially a pious one. The Westie in question happens to be a born-again evangelical.

I shamble off my porch toward the beach. Oh, what can that banging *be?* I do not need to ask as the overtime Mexicans detonate their salsa radios and continue the erection of the House of Lapham across the creek. Outer walls, inner walls, pool-house walls, gazebo walls, atrium, aquarium, arboretum, auditorium walls. Up up up. *Bang bang bang.* Olé.

"And what does Mr. Lapham require today?" I call over the water to Dave the contractor and his band of merry noise-makers. When I wish to communicate with them, I employ a cardboard megaphone purchased for that purpose at a junk shop in Eastport. Originally it was used for Harvard crew races in the late 1920s; a white *H* on a crimson horn. When the men wish to communicate with me, they use a bullhorn. These exchanges constitute most of my social life.

"Señor Moment!" cries one of the carpenters, always happy to see me for purposes of derision. They call me Señor Moment—"senior moment"—which I kind of like.

"One more floor," Dave says. He shrugs apologetically. "I don't get it either. But that's what he wants: four floors."

"Because no one else has more than three," I suggest.

Dave is too tactful to agree. "Sorry for the disruption, Harry. But we're coming to the end."

"You have no idea." That I mutter.

My name is Harry March. I am the last and least of three generations of Marches who have lived year-round on this private and once-tranquil island in once-tranquil Quogue. The first two generations, teachers and doctors, were spared rude awakenings. They reared strong and handsome families in this house, which too was strong and handsome once, as was its current resident. (You'll have to take my word for that.) Now the old place molts shingles and its shutters tilt into commas and apostrophes. The effort that some people expend to achieve the distressed look in their homes is unnecessary here. *Bang bang bang bang bang.*

"I bet you'll make a novel out of all this," says Dave. He wants me to start writing again.

"What should I call it, *Lapham Rising*?"

"You can do better than that." He smiles.

"Not these days."

It is 5:45 A.M. on my island. If there were justice in the universe at this hour, if there were justice on the East End of Long Island at this hour, I would be alone with the egrets and the cormorants drilling the water in their birdy silence. I would be alone with the tides and the swales of the dunes, also silent, and with the pines speckled by splashes of early sunlight, and with the line traced on the sea by a distant ketch—all silent. I would be alone with the oversexed ducks flying above me in their crazy syntax, and with the streaks of the reluctantly awakening red sky (sailors take warning), silent as well.

But the House of Lapham requires four floors. The House of Lapham requires a movie theater. The House of Lapham requires a state-of-the-art kitchen and a state-of-the-art toilet and a sundeck and a moon deck and a hot tub. Gaah.

3

The House of Lapham requires a master bedroom with a view to die for.

Of course, the view they will die for—Mr. and Mrs. Lapham propped up in their cherrywood sleigh bed, their heads resting against an Alp of fluffed goose-down pillows wrapped in white cases, further supported by yet more pillows encased in white shams, their safely tanned legs stretched out beneath white sheets and a white duvet in their bedroom for the master—is me. Out their Andersen triple-pane picture window they will peer, only to see Harry March on his barren island in his shapeless house, sans air conditioners, sans Belgian tiles, sans everything but life, cracked as it is. The Laphams will die for the view of the one watching them hoping that they will die for the view of the one who likewise has them as a view to die for.

Bang bang bang bang bang. Do not concern yourself. I am not barking yet. Not yet. Hector does the barking around here. Religiously.

"Hombres!" I cry to the carpenters. "Good news! I've called the INS. Soon you'll be able to ditch your girlfriends and go home to your wives and their mothers!"

They laugh, as they do every morning. "The INS eesn't up yet, Señor March." They laugh some more. When Latins speak English with that comic lilt, they sound as if they're making fun of the language. They probably are.

4

"These early starts weren't *my* idea," Dave says. "He's pushing us, and he's paying for it."

"Lapham," I say, my voice as festive as an autopsy.

"Lapham," he confirms with a sigh. "Ten months is no time at all for a job this big."

"Ten months?" I spread open my arms in mock wonderment. "Has it been only ten months?"

Dave's a good guy. I have known him for some ten years. Local, in his forties; his people once worked as housemaids and chauffeurs for families whose fortunes have long since been dissipated and whose scions, half drunk and half dressed, now shuffle around the Hamptons villages in bedroom slippers, calling to one another in loud, patrician voices absent of gender. When employed, they curate the local whaling museum; the local scrimshaw and plover museum; the paintings of whales, scrimshaw, and plovers in the local art museum; and the museum museum. Their hair is uncut. Their ancestors are recalled only in street names.

Dave, in contrast, has come up in the world, and by his own sweat. Shortish and square, he looks like a substantial piece of rope, the sort of thing mountaineers might use to keep one another alive.

He has his oldest boy, Jack, working on the crew today. Jack flicks me a wave. He is one of the few people around here from whom the mention of a movie made before last week will evoke more than the stare of the dead.

"How far away from me are you standing?" I ask Dave. It is difficult to determine distance over water.

"I don't know—two hundred feet, maybe two-fifty."

"Good."

"Why 'good'?"

I pretend not to hear him.

I ought to tell you where we are. Picture Long Island as an overfed alligator in profile, its body extending a hundred miles or so in the waters off New York City, east by northeast. The gator's jaws are open, its maw forming Peconic Bay. The waters of Long Island Sound burble above the creature's snout, between it and the Connecticut shoreline. Along the lower jaw are arranged, in an uneven line running from west to east to its farthest reach, Westhampton, my own little Quogue, Southampton, Water Mill, Bridgehampton, East Hampton, Amagansett, Montauk, and all the other towns, villages, and hamlets collectively known as the Hamptons. To the south of them, below the alligator's lower jaw, is the Atlantic; to the south of that, Brazil.

My island, called Noman, sits in a creek that runs between two mainlands. It is a sandbar, really, with yellow bushes, stunted trees, my humble home and hearth, and a choppy, sallow lawn (a product of the "driest summer in memory") leading down to a narrow pebble beach furnished with a chaise, a forest-green Adirondack chair that is slowly but definitely ruining my back, and not much of a dock.

The dock is L-shaped; from my vantage point ashore it forms an upside-down L that juts straight out into the water twenty-five feet or so, then veers to the left another fifteen feet, parallel to the beach, to complete the letter.

Noman itself is shaped like Tennessee, though it is considerably smaller. One could clearly see the outlines of Tennessee if one were to hover over the island in a helicopter or in one of those British Harrier fighter jets that take off vertically. I myself have not done so.

I named my island Noman so that when anyone asks where I live I shall tell them, and they shall say, "Where is that?" and I shall answer, "Noman is an island." To date—and it has been years—no one has asked.

On the mainland to my west is a nature preserve, an open zoo for leopard frogs, box turtles, and blue-spotted salamanders, which, because it is quiet, lovely, harmless, and there, will not be preserved much longer. That is the way in these parts. Last month, the local college was razed to make room for the construction of eighty-eight six-million-dollar homes, a development to be called Higher Education Acres. On the mainland to the east of me lies Lapham's shore, fronting what were green, moist flatlands until a couple of years ago, when the developers arrived and drooled. In the present context, my house faces the wrong side of the creek, meaning that my days, once spent in earnest if fruitless meditation, are now usurped by the delirious sounds of real estate.

"What is that thing?" Dave shouts to me over his bullhorn.

I drag the Da Vinci's pinion wheels from the end of the dock nearer the house, where the parts were dumped, to the far end, where the L angles left. Across the creek, Dave watches me warily. I shove the wheels under the black tarp that mostly conceals the rest of the stash. The tarp gives the Da Vinci the appearance of a large dormant animal with protruding humps and points, its head facing the construction site. The aft and forward crosspiece are sticking out like bandy legs.

"What *is* that thing?"

"Nothing," I tell him. "Just some driftwood. I'm thinking of building a picnic table."

"For all your formal dinner parties?"

"Or an all-weather tennis court, or a most-weather patio," I go on. "Or I may stand the beams on end and call it Woodhenge."

After speaking with me for a short while, most people stop asking questions.

On the opposite shore, the Laphams' thirty-six-thousand-square-foot castle rises on eight acres like a mutant flamingo alongside fortifications belonging to other royal pretenders just like them. The Klimers, the Courters, the McWalmarts, the Hooligans, the Caesars, the Wontons, the Rapynes, the Bolognas, and the Bonanzas—ah, the Bonanzas. I have never laid eyes on any of them, including Lapham. But he consumes my special attention because his house is the biggest and gives off the most bang for the buck, and also because his family creeps back into the gothic caves of American history. Third mates on clipper ships, assistants to slave auctioneers, pale and lascivious clergymen, disbarred magistrates, corrupt patroons, embezzler quartermasters, informers for Andrew Carnegie—a genealogy of disappointed ambition. They made money nonetheless. (In 1878, Moses Lapham of Cincinnati, in a failed effort to fashion a tooth-yanking device, inadvertently invented the asparagus tongs, which soon gave rise to escargot tongs, the grape scissors, the lobster cracker, and other instruments associated with dining and grasping.) The family continued to reproduce like inbred collies until their heads became so pointed there was no room for brains, and yet fortunately, no need.

Today, the latest of the breed, still quite wealthy thanks to untouchable trusts and the irrational though lucky investments of his forebears, is not gainfully employed. Lapham's occupation is a Web site he created, on which he offers

America his opinions both on current events and on life in general, called Lapham's Aphms. He either seems to have misunderstood or misspelled *aphorisms*. The English language, though his own, presents him with challenges. Yet he shows great self-confidence. One of Lapham's aphms is: "He who does not promote himself will never be promoted." He is currently said to be at work on a memoir titled *Lapham Is Here*. As if that were in question.

Wealth heaped on wealth, nor truth nor safety buys, / The dangers gather as the treasures rise: Dr. Johnson wrote that, and Dr. Johnson was always right.

"Señor March!"

"What is it, José?" The day they began work over there, I called out "José," figuring that at least one of them had to claim the name. José looks like a young Ricardo Montalban, debonair even in overalls three sizes too big. Today he and I are chummy, a model of exuberant and mutually baffled Anglo-Latino relations.

"What happened to your ear?" he asks me. The gauze pad I hurriedly taped to it after Hector's morning greeting makes it appear that I have a brand-new tennis ball wedged into the side of my head.

"It fell off from your hammering."

"Forgeeve us, señor. When we finish with Mr. Lapham, we will come over and build a house for you."

"I already have a house," I tell him stupidly.

"Oh," he says with a laugh, staring straight at it. "We couldn't tell."

In short, the situation in which I find myself—as you may have detected—is not yet perfect, a bit up for grabs.

My ear hurts. And my back hurts. And no one plays Blossom Dearie anymore. And no one remembers Junior Gilliam anymore. And I haven't written a word in eight years, much less eight words in one year, yet I watch *Murder She Wrote* four times a day when I'm not otherwise occupied, as I currently am. And my wife couldn't take me anymore and now lives in Beverly Hills with an event planner named Joel. I have memorialized our many happy years together with a life-size stone statue of her seated at the kitchen table reading the *New York Times* and yet, because she is a statue, never telling me to wait till I hear this, or predicting that I won't believe that. (The statue was commissioned from a sculptor in New Hampshire, a Hungarian dwarf with massive hands and a hair-trigger temper. I liked him at once.) And my children, who amazingly enough still love me, had the horse sense to grow into adults and move elsewhere. And I look like hell in my ten-year-old rat-gray shorts and my navy-blue polo shirt with the hole the size of a half-dollar where I cut out the polo player and my Tevas with the tired Velcro. And the Da Vinci awaits completion by nightfall. I have a lecture to finish by nightfall as well. And the Mexicans have just turned up the volume on "She Bangs."

But at least I have Lapham, my neighbor Lapham, conspicuously consuming my creek, my birds, my salt marshes, my island, my country, my life. Up, up, and up he rises. And I again am reminded, as if I needed reminding, that I do not fit in the world. Good thing I do not live on it.

Two

Nice ear," says Hector. It is 8:23, and he has deigned to uncurl and emerge from the house onto the porch, where I am at work. I creak in my wicker rocker, which sheds flakes with each creak, and take notes on a legal pad, raising it to block his view of my face. I try to ignore him. He doesn't care.

"Why don't you go and talk to God?" I ask him, without looking up or down. He entered the world a Scottish Presbyterian, as I assume all Westies do. But then he found a "more personal God" in what I have come to think of as the Church of the Holy Terrier. If he was difficult to live with before, he has been impossible since.

"How's the lecture coming?" he asks insincerely.

"Fine, fine." I keep taking notes, hoping he will wander off somewhere to stare fixedly at a daisy or a pebble. Eventually he does, happy in the knowledge that he has interrupted me.

But he always turns back with a parting shot. "Two earth-shattering projects in a single day! My goodness! You're a multitasker, that's what you are!"

He is opposed to both undertakings, the Da Vinci and the lecture. The lecture, on the meaning of the twentieth century, is to be presented at the Chautauqua Institution tomorrow morning, twenty-six hours from now. I've just begun working on it. I'm glad I didn't put it off till the last minute.

"We're devoting a week to the twentieth century," said the chief Chautauquan in his phone call some ten months ago. He had the voice of the nonprofit CEO—liquid clarity trembling with hope, which at any other time I would have dashed at once. I keep a mental portfolio of rare diseases from which I suffer whenever I am threatened with a social experience, and I was about to share with Mr. Chautauqua the melancholy news of my scurvy. But his call arrived on the very day that Laphamworld received its first Big Bang. I read the coincidence as a sign, and of the two events I forged my mission.

"An entire week?"

"Yes, it's a tall order," he went on earnestly, evidently assuming that I still dwelt among normal people who said normal things. "But I thought we'd break it down into special subjects: twentieth-century art, politics, science, and so forth."

In my former life, I used to give readings from time to time at Chautauqua's upstate summer utopia, but I would stay only a day and not one second longer. That was as much of institutionalized sublimity as I could bear, of watching the worthy citizens patrol the grounds licking ice cream cones and waving to one another in a smiley somnambulism, as in movies about heaven in which candidates await their ascension. Yet these were, I knew, good, decent, modest, temperate folks. They used words such as *supportive* but were otherwise admirable.

"And what do you want me to talk about?" I asked him.

"The whole thing."

"The whole century? Well, I hope you've allotted me a good fifteen minutes."

"We thought a novelist, a creative thinker like yourself, might find an unusual approach."

Respectability is a curse, take it from me. I have found that a good reputation is much more difficult to shake than a bad one. People do not forgive respectability. Despite the fact that I stopped writing long ago, and despite my, shall we say, distinctive behavior, I continue even now to receive invitations to speak or read from my books.

"Of course, you're welcome to bring Mrs. March."

"I would, but she's getting a bit heavy to carry around."

Give us the meaning of the twentieth century, will you do that? called the Chautauquans from their lacy red-and-blue porches stuffed with gladiolas, and their leafy glade and their true blue lake and their bell tower out of *Vertigo* and their hotel out of *The Shining*, and their largest outdoor pipe organ in the world, and their poorly concealed caches of booze forbidden by the original founding Methodists. Will you do that for us? No problem, I said.

The twentieth century! One hundred years of progress! Edison becomes Freud becomes Einstein becomes Lapham. Yeats becomes Picasso becomes Stravinsky becomes Lapham. Silas Lapham becomes Lapham, too—the difference between William Dean Howells's arriviste protagonist (who also built a big house, in Boston) and the newer version across the creek being that in early America, money alone could not buy social position, while today who cares?

Well, that's my lecture, Chautauquans. You've been a wonderful audience. I'm here till Doomsday.

"Have you laid out your Lapham theory yet?" Hector asks from a hole he has just dug in the damp sand for typically purposeless amusement. He trains his little black eyes on me as I write. "About how Lapham represents all that's wrong with modern civilization? That's my favorite part."

"Keep digging, Mr. Tail." I sometimes call him that to remind him of his place in the animal hierarchy. "You haven't hit six feet yet."

"You're such a cliché," he says. "A recluse on an island, railing against his times."

"*I'm* a cliché? And what do you call a talking dog?"

He extends himself in the Westie stretch—rump raised, front lowered, and with an expression of ludicrous complacency. "You know what you need? You need a little religion in your life. Why don't you come to church with me sometime?"

"I'm too tall to get in the door."

"If only you could see it, my wonderful megachurch. Three thousand terriers, all clapping and howling and standing on their hind legs together—I tell you, it's a miracle, that's what it is." I drum my fingers on the arm of the rocker and wait for his ecstasy to wane. "I'll pray for you," he says.

"You do that."

Across the creek, the Mexicans have added the screech of an electric saw to the symphony of their hammering. One of them is singing, "Yi yi yi yi, in China they eat it with chili"— for my benefit, I am certain. Hector's ears snap up at the "music," and he decides to compete with it, also for my benefit. He has a terrible singing voice, all sharps, and loud: "Amazing grace, how sweet the sound . . ."

"Do you mind!"

"Oh, so you're the only one who can sing around here?"

"As a matter of fact, yes."

He turns his back on me and kicks sand in my direction.

I confess, there have been times in the past few days when I have thought of not going through with either the lecture or the Da Vinci. So much to risk, so much to lose. Retreating to the suburbs of thought, I figured, why bother, and began to listen to the blandishments of a coward's conscience. But this morning my resolve is unbending. Somewhere beneath the noise and the smoke and the blight and the barbaric squalor lies a world worth excavating—a world worth fighting for. One must try, don't you agree? One must make the effort.

"I just love the Hamptons." Hector heaves an ingenue's sigh to ensure I'll notice. He fears that my plot will jeopardize our ability to keep living out here, and he is right. Now he is beside me on the porch, his muzzle raised toward the sky, his eyes closed in a demiswoon.

"And why is that, Mr. Tail?"

" 'Why is that?' Only *you* would ask such a question. The ocean, the beaches, the history, the light! God's bounty everywhere."

"And the traffic?"

"That doesn't bother me."

"And the fakery? The empty chatter? The gossip? The ostentation? The excess?"

He has mentioned history not because he knows any, ancient or modern, but because he thinks it will appeal to my backward-leaning disposition. It does not. My assessment of people in every century, with the glorious exception of the moderate, modest, enlightened, levelheaded yet courageous eighteenth, is equally unfavorable. All eras, I am certain, have produced the same proportion of goofs, dunces, and malefactors—87 to 91 percent—no matter whether they were adding a fourth floor to their summer palace or a fourth outhouse to their dingy saltbox. Only the Indians, who constituted the Hamptons' history until the Dutch and English civilized them to death, showed signs of having any sense or wit. In what was clearly a blast of clairvoyance, they named the settlement around Bridgehampton Saggabonac, which means "the place of nut grounds."

Yet he is right about the beauty of the area. If it were possible to subtract people like the Laphams from the Hamptons, this would be quite a pleasant place. Those ducks, for example, that whet out in arrowhead formations over the Atlantic, and the glib gulls, and the oaten dunes flecked with tufts of sea grass grading into gold, and the ocean herself that gushes in response to approaching rain, and the beach that contorts to the shapes of angels on tombstones, awls, hunchbacks, lovers lying thigh to thigh, and the flotsam from a mackerel schooner that still bears the stench of the catch . . .

The red sky has paled to a Wedgwood blue, but it is fooling no one. There will be a storm this evening, bet on it. It will be a lollapalooza. We islanders can always tell. We can tell because they said so on morning TV. Between the news bulletins trumpeting the latest medical discovery (drinking water causes urination) and the latest political analysis (the candidate who gets the most votes is likely to win), the preternaturally hepped-up weather people promised a doozy. A summer storm over Lapham's monstrosity, arriving at the moment for which I have been planning for months. A night on Bald Mountain. The prospect pleases me.

And where is Lapham himself at this hour? I wonder. Guffawing over the telephone at the tepid joke of some yes-man in his employ, about the parrot who walks into a bar? Reveling in a tidbit of flattery deployed by the oily butler? Spooning his granola into an oversize bowl glazed in Florence expressly for him? Flossing? Gaah. Composing an aphm? Smiling at the new day like a rancid pancake? And why am I thinking about him? That is the crime, you see. I am thinking about Lapham. Not a year ago, at this time of morning, I would have been thinking about Dr. Johnson or of Ida Lupino in *High Sierra*, or of chomping on lobster rolls in Ipswich, Massachusetts, or my first girlfriend, Claire—whose breasts grew so large that she bowed like a Japanese businessman as she walked, but who was nonetheless very sweet and very smart—or of nothing at all. And now?

I lay down my legal pad.

"All done?" Hector asks, knowing that I am not. I do not answer him. "Shouldn't you be getting the Da Vinci ready?" He thinks if he can shuttle me between the two tasks, I will fail to complete either one.

But I was about to set aside the lecture anyway, since it is the easier of the two projects and if necessary I can wing it, and since it will work only if the Da Vinci also works. First things first.

"Harry!" Dave calls to me over the bullhorn. "We're going to have a big blow in a little while. It'll sound like dynamite, but it's OK. I just thought I should prepare you."

"I can't wait."

"On the brighter side, it's nearly Kathy Time. Jack tells me it's his favorite time of day." The boy smiles shyly at his father's ribbing. "We'll be taking a break."

As will I. Everyone takes a break at Kathy Time.

In the meantime, though, I return to the dock. I carry the forward crosspiece and the spindle heads over to the tarp and crawl under. So far, I have done most of the work at night, out of earshot and away from the prying eyes of Dave and his crew. Because of the narrow space between the Da Vinci and the edge of the dock where it becomes the L, I have had to be careful, maneuvering on all fours and holding the flashlight in my mouth. It has not been easy.

But now I am nearly there. I fit the mortises and test the ropes and the frame. I slip the point of the hook into the eye of the bolt. The trigger requires a knot, a bowline, which I forget for a moment how to tie. What's that ditty about where to make the loops? "The rabbit comes out of the hole," I recite aloud. "Goes round the tree and runs back down the hole again."

"What rabbit?" asks Hector, looking as ferocious as a corn muffin.

I tie the bowline. I tug at the burlap pouch. The ball of pinewood is progressing nicely, though because it is the size of a medicine ball, I had to squeeze it down into the tub. All that remains is to fit the rollers to the plates and attach the skein winch and the winch spanner.

"Don't forget the horsehair," says Hector. Not that I would. I leave the dock, and head back up the lawn. He follows, sniffing as if he were searching for drugs in a suitcase.

For some reason, he has taken a particular interest in the fact that I have opted to include genuine horsehair in the Da Vinci's construction. I simply wanted to be authentic. The original plans drawn up by Sir Ralph Payne-Gallwey in 1903, for which I sent away and have followed to the letter except as to scale, specified the use of horsehair for the torsion spring. So I phoned the people who run the Bridgehampton Classic horse show to ask if they had any horsehair to spare. They hung up on me. Then I phoned the stables in the neighboring town of Quiogue and asked, "Next time you take your horses to the barber, may I have the clippings?" They sent over a basketful without comment.

Carefully I extract the horsehair from the large Mason jar in which I have been storing it, atop the one small hill on Noman.

"Can I help?" says Hector. I would ask "How?" but that would prolong the conversation.

Grasping one end of the sheaf of hair in each hand, I rotate my fists in opposite circles and slowly twist it, as the diagram indicated. It rolls easily, then springs back to its original state. I twist it again. I do this twice a day to maintain its bounce and torque.

Why do I keep it in a jar on a hill? Because that is what Wallace Stevens wrote about doing in "Anecdote of a Jar." He set down his jar on a hill in Tennessee, and Noman is shaped like Tennessee, and just as Stevens's jar brought order to the "slovenly wilderness" of its surroundings, so my jar of horsehair, too, when put to proper use, will effect the imposition of order on my immediate surroundings, and indeed beyond, the same kind of order that the eighteenth century could have brought to the slovenly wilderness of the twentieth, had it not had the misfortune to precede it. I trust that is clear.

"Señor March!" cries José from the other side of the creek. "You look like a conquistador on that heel!"

"If I were a conquistador, guess where you'd be?"

"Where all the conquistadors are now." He laughs. "What are you doing?"

I interpose my body between him and the jar, though he's probably too far away too see it anyway. "Searching for serenity," I tell him. "Trying to be where Lapham is not."

He swings his arm in a slow arc, as if presenting the universe to eighth graders at the planetarium. "But Señor Lapham is everywhere!" *Bang bang bang bang bang.*

Would that he were speaking figuratively. Every time I take my eyes off the construction site, it seems to double its size, as though it were an endlessly enlarging mythical animal—one of those terrible Greek freak creations born of the forced copulation of a god with an animal, the god of cathedral ceilings or of mansard roofs with a toucan or a buffalo—producing a vague composite with indefinite haunches and misty tentacles; head of owl; horn of gnu; torso of panther; gills, claws, trunks; the tail of a langur; the feet of a fruit bat; a hundred legs splayed in a hundred different directions, the body parts continually ejected and becoming independent structures, outbuildings, each individually terrible yet bearing a ghastly resemblance to the mother animal. When the house is completed, will it expand of its own accord? In the middle of the night, will I be awakened by the bubble-bursts of skin, the popping of limbs and of eyes from their sockets, the elongation of a telescopic wing, and the screeching, the agonized screeching, of growing pains?

Hector eyes me as though I were a squirrel eyeing *him.*

"And by the way," he says, "just where do your two little proj-ects leave *me*?" No matter how holy he may sound, he is driven solely by self-interest.

"Don't worry, I'll take you to Chautauqua. You won't be abandoned."

"And what if I don't *want* to go to Chautauqua?"

"Well, I can leave you here to deal with the police. You can explain what I did. They'll doubtless arrest you as an accom-plice."

"Not me," he says. "I won't say a word. I'll just look cute and bewildered. 'Oh, where is my master? Why did he desert me?' Poor little doggie." He goes through his curriculum of head tilts, including the Adorable; the What's-Going-On?; the You-Must-Be-Kidding; the Quizzical (representing gen-uine confusion); and his choice of the moment, the Forlorn.

"That's why you're coming with me," I tell him. "I don't want to leave any witnesses. Besides, you'll enjoy hearing me lecture."

"What a treat. And you know how I love treats."

"Of course, if you want to stay behind and learn how to fill your own water bowl and buy dog food for yourself . . ."

"Bite me," he says.

I've tried.

Three

Ten A.M.: Kathy Time. Time for Kathy Polite to take off her clothes. She spells her surname Polite but pronounces it "pole-EET," to add that continental *je ne sais quoi* to her uniquely successful real estate operation. Whenever I talk with her, which is as infrequently as possible, I make a point of pretending not to know how she pronounces her name, and I replace it with that adjective of courtesy that mocks her existence.

"That's Pole-EET, as you perfectly well know, you old coot." She always speaks to me coquettishly, as though she had just returned from Savannah to her favorite old uncle's plantation, and is capable of reducing me to blushes and stumbles with the droop of an eyelid.

"Ah'm so sorry! I was just being polite."

"Ah don't know why Ah waste one word on you!" She puckers her lips like a grouper. "Ah'll never sell you *anything,* you old skinflint."

"That is *SKINE*-flint," I correct her. "And Ah would gladly purchase one of your delightful Taras, Miss Pole-EET, but the cotton crop has been so po' this year, we've had to eat the slaves."

That I would never buy so much as a lean-to from Kathy has had no impact, I hardly need to report, on her booming real estate business. Alongside the hundreds of "gems," "steps to the ocean," "priced to sell," and "just bring your toothbrush" houses for which she shills on both overladen jaws of Long Island, she also represents what grotesqueries are still for sale around Lapham's. She did not sell that particular magnificence, of course: Lapham had his own broker (a roommate from St. Mark's) and his own personal architect, an in-law of Albert Speer's, whose firm has been in the family for generations, and which had erected the dank mossy manses in Newport and Saratoga, as well as several more recent, bright mausoleums in Florida and Wyoming, near the Snake River—where, it is said, the whitefish committed a Jim Jones mass suicide in response.

But, as Lapham rises, Kathy is not far behind. Mainly she sells spec houses to Lapham wannabes, of whom there seems to be an endless parade. Thus, though without a contract, and herself but dimly aware of it, she is Lapham's silent partner in the destruction of the universe. She once told me that she was—and I quote—"very grateful to Mr. Lapham for setting the proper standard of architectural elegance in the area. As yet, Ah have not made his acquaintance. But on the day that Ah am so fortunate, Ah shall shake his hand warmly and tell him, 'It is people like you, suhr, who make the Hamptons the Hamptons.'"

Were it not for Kathy Time, I would have gutted her on the spot.

"Hah," she calls from her boat this morning—"Hah" being a conjunction of "Hi" and a sigh.

"Hah," I call back. She wants to assure herself that I am watching. She need not worry. I walk down to the platform of the dock facing the creek to decrease the distance between us, and improve my view. One does what one can.

She surveys me with a fatalistic shrug, as if I were a decision she regretted. "Harry, you need some new clothes."

I would say, "And you do not," but I don't wish to delay her from her appointed rounds.

On the stroke of ten, this is what she does every sweet drifty summer day. And here she is again, with her forty-year-old diver's body, standing like a soft little piece of vertical caramel in the bow of her Grady White with the dual 250-horsepower gunmetal-gray Yamaha engines lying at rest. The powerboat is anchored midway between Noman

ROGER ROSENBLATT

and Lapham's shore. It throbs. Who would not? I see her, clear as starlight, reaching for the heavens and stretching herself like some living figurehead on the prow of a New Bedford whaler.

On each side of her boat, port as well as starboard, facing both my island and the long line of developed and developing houses across from me, is a large red-painted sign: "Polite for the Elite, Realtors." The lettering is thick, high, and three-dimensional. One could read it from miles offshore. I imagine that the signs allow her to write off the boat as a business expense. But the real, unforgettable, visually in-eradicable advertisement is Kathy herself, out for her regular morning swim.

She has been skinny-dipping off her boat for nine glorious summers. And there is hardly a man around here—including those who drive over for the occasion from as far away as Shirley and Mattituck, and including all the *-ogues* on both alligator jaws: Patch-, Cutch-, Haupp-, Aquab-, as well as Qui- and Qu- who does not stop whatever else he is doing at precisely ten o'clock to gaze in appreciative wonder at the wonder of Kathy Polite.

"Hah, Hector!" He scampers down to the water's edge and makes a snowy flurry of greeting her. His manner with people other than me is to rush toward them exhibiting a frantic eagerness, wagging and levitating, as if he were a kidnap victim signaling for rescue.

"Hah, boys!" she calls to Dave and his men. Dave and Jack give her a decorous wave from the waist. The Mexicans are more demonstrative.

In her way, she is a genius. Other realtors in the area spend a fortune on brochures advertising houses that are "this side of Paradise," or that offer "location, location," or that were "built in a unique style by the owner," meaning that they were designed by someone on whom German silent horror films made an indelible impression. The brokers need to print updates every week, because all of these houses sell in a snap and are immediately replaced by new listings. It is expensive to produce the brochures, and it takes both time and effort to distribute them around the sidewalks in front of the cheese shops and the basket shops and the shops that sell photographs of other shops, and to place them in the doorways of the "We have mahimahi!" restaurants, where they lie in stacks and gather sand.

What Kathy figured out was that it would be much more convenient, not to say more consonant with her own taste and character, if instead of having to seek out customers, she could devise an activity that would entice *them* to come to *her*. So without using a flyer, posters, a Web site with "such a cute name dot-com," or any other instruments of modern publicity, she attached her signs to her boat and began the practice of her mute morning sales pitch. She was, and is, her own Open House.

"Why don't you join me today, Wrinkles?" she calls from the side deck.

"No time," I shout back. "I have to water my duck."

"Your WHAT?" She clamps a hand to her mouth as if shocked. The last time Kathy was shocked was when her cousin said no. She heard me, all right. I say the same thing to her every day.

"What's wrong with your ear, Harry? Did you pull a Van Gogh?"

"Yes, Buttercup, I cut it off as a gesture of my love for you. Actually, I was trying to cut my throat."

"Not if Ah get there first. And what *is* that under the tarp? It looks quite sinister—much lahk yourself, Harry March." She often says my first and last names together, as if she were addressing and classifying me in the same breath. She presents two even rows of large, newly whitened teeth.

The front of the Da Vinci lies to my right. A portion of the aft crosspiece is still showing. I cover it. "Why don't you just go on with your morning's work?" I try not to sound too eager.

She preens on her deck, her face as cute as neon. She turns

first to the left, then to the right, as a much-honored actress might do onstage: the first lady of real estate, acknowledging an audience she cannot see but knows is out there. Distracted, she slips out of her green top and her beige shorts, displaying panties and a bra as white as glaciers against her autobronzed skin, which is russet-colored, or the color of unpolished gold. With the ceremonial prance of a Lipizzaner, she walks to the bow. She walks to the stern. Then to the bow. Then to the stern. Onshore, hedges jostle. Car windows open. Rabbits stiffen. Back to the bow. Back to the stern.

At last she is still again, and—as if lost in an ethereal reverie concerning plummeting interest rates or some newly minted millionaire just in from Rahway—she unhooks her bra and drops it at her side like a lace handkerchief. She looks out at the water. She looks at the shore. The shore's mouth is dry and agape. Now she slips off her panties. One can almost hear a sighing of the clouds. But there are no clouds.

"Why do you stare like that every morning?" asks Hector.

"You wouldn't understand." I never mention his first medical procedure.

She touches her forehead, then reaches up into her hair, a braid of browns and oranges that swings down to the middle of her back. She loosens the braid, and out spills plenty's horn. She touches her ribs and rubs them as if attempting to induce wings. She glows like a coal in ash. Though I would have no way of knowing this, I would put her normal body temperature at about 106. The water will hiss when she enters it. Though I would have no way of knowing this either, I imagine that she initiates lovemaking by leaping on a man from a great height, say a hayloft or a chandelier, and whispering "Surprise!" She touches her thighs and her knees as she steps to the side of the boat away from me and facing Lapham's. Now she straightens her body. Now she perches. Now she dives. The water opens its grateful arms and waits.

At this moment of her diving, as she is suspended in mid-jackknife, nothing happens on the East End of Long Island. Not a single nail is nailed. Not a single hedge is trimmed. Not a single bottle of Château Whatanamazingwine is sold. Not one compliment is paid to a tomato or an ear of corn or a peach. No one asks where the potato fields have gone. Likewise the duck farms. No Filipino housekeeper is yelled at for failing to position the fruit forks correctly. No year-round resident is pushed aside at a farmers' market. No one asks anyone else to a small dinner just for close friends, or wishes there were more time to spend reading quietly on the beach away from all the big parties. No one gives kudos. Or draws raves. No one embarks on an exciting new phase of his life, or enters the third act of his life, or comments that life is a journey. No one plans a benefit dinner dance for a fatal disease. No one lowers his voice to say "Jew."

Nothing moves. Nothing makes a sound. The universe lies in respectful silence as sex and commerce find their apogee in Kathy Polite and her morning swim. For one brief moment in this day, for what *certainly* will be the *only* such moment, I am at peace—all bitterness relieved, all burdens lifted from me. The wind kicks up. I bless her unaware.

Four

It may surprise you to learn that I have considerable difficulty performing the ordinary transactions of daily living. Having my home on Noman allows me to avoid those transactions generally. But there are times when I am forced by circumstance to live as others do, and at such times, I am reminded that there exists a sort of natural selection process that applies to one's chosen place on earth. I live on an island because I have trouble making connections. One reason I became a writer is that a writer's connections with people are made at long distance. Now I've given up even that. I would seek therapy, but I do not want to connect with an analyst.

So I have put off making my travel arrangements to Chautauqua until this, the very last minute, because I am bound to mess up those arrangements, to misunderstand what people have told me to do, or to leave home without my tickets or the papers required for my identification, or to try to check in at the wrong airline at the wrong airport, or, failing all that, to board the wrong plane headed for the wrong destination.

"I don't suppose you have a seat on a flight to Buffalo late tonight," I say to the lady from USAir who finally picks up after two minutes of automated responses.

"Why do you put it that way?"

"Because I really do not want to go to Buffalo. Tonight or any night."

"So why do it?" She sounds down-to-earth.

"I've agreed to make the trip. A deal's a deal."

"That's honorable of you. I'm sure the people of Buffalo will appreciate it. Where are you now?"

"In Quogue."

"The Hamptons. I've never been. It sounds exciting."

"Excitement plus," I murmur.

"All those parties!"

"That appeals to you?"

"I don't know. But just reading about the Hamptons' social life makes it seem like it goes on nonstop."

She is correct. A mathematician who visited the Springs section of East Hampton a couple of summers ago, and who evidently had no more pressing use for his years of training, decided to quantify the social activity of the Hamptons. In the hundred-day season covering the usual stretch from the end of May through the first week of September, he counted roughly 26,000 scheduled social events, for an average of 260 in any twenty-four-hour period. These included bona fide parties (brunch, lunch, dinner, private, club, birthday [surprise and non-surprise], anniversary, theme, and book), fund-raisers (political, medical, ecological, institutional), dances, artists' shows, walkathons, boat races, softball games, wine tastings, official celebrations (Memorial Day, the Fourth of July, Labor Day), and other, miscellaneous gatherings ranging from the poorly attended picnic held on July 9 to commemorate the halfway point between the Fourth and Bastille Day (at which guests gather to read the Declaration of Independence aloud in French) to the wildly popular re-creation of *Moby-Dick* (wherein an inflatable white plastic whale with happy eyes is floated in East Hampton's Three Mile Harbor while participants attempt to harpoon it with broomsticks and holler, "He heaps me!").

The mathematician, who also happened to be clinically depressed, further calculated that the average Hamptons resident slept for approximately seven and a half hours a night, leaving sixteen and a half hours in which to accomplish everything else. Doing the math, he determined that per individual, some four hours a day were devoted to eating, and other bodily necessities, which left twelve and a half hours for "interpersonal activities." Eventually, he went a bit overboard and attempted to inventory the kisses of greeting and departure bestowed on various occasions, breaking them down into one cheek and two, and then the number of times Tuscany was mentioned in a given week, also "gravitas," "counterintuitive," and "scenario." But the amounts proved overwhelming. At the end of that summer, he found a different use for his own free time: he committed seppuku with a seafood shish-kebab skewer, standing next to a seven-thousand-dollar Viking outdoor grill offered for sale on the sidewalk outside the Loaves and Fishes culinary supplies store in Bridgehampton. Friends now gather for an annual cookout in his memory.

Bang bang bang bang bang.

"What's that noise?" The USAir lady sounds alarmed. I tend to forget that what has become the soundtrack of my life may be shocking to others.

"That noise is the reason I'm escaping."

"To Buffalo?" She is appropriately incredulous.

"Chautauqua—I'm actually going to Chautauqua."

She seems to be considering something. "You don't need to fly to Buffalo to get to Chautauqua. You could fly to Jamestown, New York. There's a small airport there, and it's much closer to where you're headed."

"A small airport suggests planes that are also small," I offer, more nervously than logically.

"That's true—the planes *are* small. But so are the ones to Buffalo."

"You mean you don't fly jets to Buffalo?" I distinctly remember that on previous visits, I flew up on big jets that did not crash.

"I don't like flying," says Hector, sticking his black nose into the conversation.

"Then it's fortunate that you're unable to do it," I tell him.

"We used to use jets," says the lady. "But you know how things are."

"No, I don't. How are they?"

"Nothing ever changes for the better." Her voice carries the warm breeze of the British West Indies.

I often find that I prefer speaking with disembodied intelligences to having face-to-face encounters. For many years, before I stopped writing, I worked with a book editor with whom I never conversed except on the phone. She dealt with me by phone and I with her, and we spoke only when necessary. Over those years we developed a close and trusting relationship based solely on the ways our minds corresponded and diverged. If ever we had happened to be standing inches from each other in an elevator in an office building, or on a subway platform, and not spoken, we neither of us would have had the merest clue as to who the other person was, nor probably would have shown any interest in finding out. And had we been looking at each other when we were discussing my manuscripts, we undoubtedly would have forfeited effectiveness and exactitude for the sake of courtesy or kindness or some other gesture of social compromise. But without visual distractions, we got along swimmingly, and my work was the better for it.

"Yes," I agree with the USAir lady. "Most change is for the worse. But exactly how much worse are the planes to Buffalo?" Hector shudders and begins to pray aloud.

"The Jamestown flights originate in Pittsburgh," she says, "so you'd have to go there first. And the planes are very small, only a little larger than puddle-jumpers. Eight passengers plus the pilot."

"I'm glad the pilot goes along." She chuckles politely. "And the Buffalo planes?"

"Turboprops." She quickly adds, "They're quite safe. The flight time is a bit longer than with a jet, but I'm told that the planes themselves are very comfortable."

"But perhaps you're all full up?" A small plane plummets in my head (the engine sputters, the propeller freezes, we sit knees-to-chest as the fuselage scrapes the topmost branches of the cedars). I tried, Chautauquans, but I could not book transportation. I tried for weeks. There must be something big going on in Buffalo. The annual Beef-on-Wek Festival,

the "How Many Inches of Snow Did We Have Last Winter?"
conference.

"Do you know that you have a peculiar way of speaking to
people?" she asks unnecessarily. Her tone is not accusatory.
She sounds more like a nurse. I picture her delicately maneuvering through a hospital ward in World War I, wearing a
crisp white cap with a red cross in the center, and stopping to
read letters to mutilated, homesick doughboys.

"I've always been peculiar. It's nothing personal. To you, I
mean." The reason I speak to people the way I do is that I tend
to take everything I hear literally, and I pay what turns out to
be a destructive measure of attention to the spoken word.

"You're not married." She is sure of her conclusion. "I
hope you won't mind my asking."

"You didn't ask," I remind her helpfully.

"I don't mean to be rude."

"You don't know what rude is. But why do you surmise that
I am not married?"

"I wonder," says Hector.

She hesitates. "You seem too . . . independent." I appreciate the ellipses.

"I used to be married," I tell her. Then I plunge into that
song from *The King and I:* "I had a love of my own like yours, /
I had a love of my own!" I nail the latter line and hold the
note. There follows a long pause. "Yes," I go on at last. "I was

married. To prove it, I have a life-size statue of my wife seated at our kitchen table reading the *New York Times*. She is in stone, and so is the *Times*."

A longer silence this time. "You keep a statue of your wife in your house? Is she dead?"

"Oh, no. Alive and kicking. These days she reads the *Times* with an event planner named Joel in Beverly Hills. I told the sculptor to put Chloe in shorts and a T-shirt, the way she liked to dress, and to position her comfortably and give her a rapt expression. The statue solidifies our relationship. It proves that some things *are* set in stone. Now she has the life she liked best with me, buried in the news."

"I gather you disapproved of her interest in the news."

"As she disapproved of my *lack* of interest. It was a fair exchange. I especially disapproved of the *New York Times*. 'The *New York Times* brings the world into your home every day'—need I say more?"

"Don't you think the world is worth seeing?" she asks.

" 'Worth seeing, but not worth *going* to see.' " I am quoting Dr. Johnson's retort when Boswell chided him for not wishing to accompany him on a trip to Scotland. Did the doctor not think Scotland was worth seeing? he'd demanded. I cite the reference for her and explain that Dr. Johnson was always right.

She seems to recognize that it would be prudent to return

to the matter at hand. "We have plenty of seats to Buffalo on the eleven P.M. flight. How many do you want?"

"One for myself." Then, wondering if it will queer the deal, I add, "And one for my dog." Hector's ears prick up in alarm.

"I love dogs," she says.

"Name your price."

"The dog will have to travel in the baggage compartment. But that's perfectly safe too." Amazing what gentlenesses total strangers are capable of. "Do you want me to book your return reservations now?"

I have been afraid of that question. I have tried to put off thinking about what will happen *after* Chautauqua. Once I do what I shall do this evening, what then? A moment's moral elation; a nighttime escape by rowboat to a safe haven; a hired car to take me to LaGuardia and USAir; the dreaded turboprop to Buffalo, where I shall be met at midnight by a Chautauqua driver who wants to talk to me about all the famous people he has driven since 1931—"really famous, not like you." No sleep. The certain knowledge that the police are hunting for me, and the certain pleasure that they will never think to look in Chautauqua, either because they have never heard of it or because it is so hard to get to that it lies outside every jurisdiction and has no extradition treaty with the Hamptons. The morning lecture. Followed by a life of hiding and running. Loneliness, despair, memories of chicken-fried steak at Applebee's in

Riverhead and of clambering atop the White Duck landmark when I was a kid, and bellowing quacks. Disgrace and eventual death in the cheapest room of the cheapest motel outside Bridgeport. Then interment in some potter's field that is about to be sold to a developer. Of course, I could always live out my days in upstate New York, but I would prefer to be buried horizontally and underground.

So I tell her yes, I will want return tickets for Hector and me. Yes, I will be coming home to face the music. Anyway, I *want* to face the music. Why commit an act of social protest, of civil or uncivil disobedience, if one is not prepared to suffer the consequences? Suffering the consequences is the whole point.

"Don't you think so?" I ask her. "Don't you think that if someone does something on principle, pure principle, and that something happens to break the law, he should willingly pay for the act as a public statement of his noble intentions, and as a sign of his respect for the law in general?"

"It depends on how bad the act is."

"Well, it's bad, but it's not as bad as acts get."

"The question is still too general for me to offer an opinion. I hope you're not planning to make your public statement on your flight." She is gravely serious.

"Oh, no," I tell her. "That would be crazy."

Five

I miss Chloe," says Hector out of the blue. He is staring at her statue.

"No, you don't. You couldn't stand her. And she felt the same way about you."

"She adored me," he says with a straight face, which is all he has. "And I felt very warmly toward her."

I make a few more notes for the Chautauqua lecture, then head for the dock again to adjust the winches. The assembly is nearly complete. I am glad I chose the Da Vinci model. Sir Ralph's plans also provided schematics for the Bellifortis, the Stirling, and the War Wolf, whose name I found darkly appealing. But in the end I selected the Da Vinci because it looked so clean, so purposeful in the pictures, and even more so as it has come together under the tarp.

"Have it your way," I tell Hector. It is 11:09. *Tick tock, tick tock*. He follows a few paces behind me. An outsider observing us would conclude that we represented the heartwarming tableau of man and his best and most loyal friend.

"The thing about Chloe," he goes on, emboldened by the fact that I want to drop the topic, "was that she lived in the world, she made plans, she talked to everybody. With Chloe, we had a little life around here."

"A little too much for my taste."

"So why did you marry her?"

"Because she had a lovely soul. Still does."

"Then why did *she* marry *you*?"

"She mistook the occasional normalities in my fiction for the life I preferred." But why am I spilling all this to Cujo? "I have an idea!" I tell him. "Why don't you revert to type and dig up a bone or something? Or maybe create a meal out of your own vomit?"

"You're a misanthrope," he says. "You hate everyone."

In fact, I am not a misanthrope, though I do not bother to protest the characterization. I like certain, select individuals. I even have a few friends distributed across America and Europe, two in Africa, and one in Asia Minor, with whom I exchange greetings once every three or four years, which is how we remain friends. I bear no one ill will, except Lapham. I am perfectly content to watch others go happily about their business, unless one of those others is Lapham. I also was perfectly content to see my family—Chloe and the children—go happily about *their* business in the great wide world. It did not matter that what seemed great and wide to them was alien territory to me.

But watching those others, my family included, always felt to me like viewing a painting on a museum wall—one of those 1890s New England winter scenes, in which boys and girls skate on a glassy pond and their parents, swathed in colorful scarves, haul sleds through the thick snow. I was entranced by such paintings, pleased to see any segment of the race engaged in civilized play; I wished the participants well. And when it came to my own family, I wished them well too. I did my best to ensure their well-being. I just never wanted to be part of the picture.

Hector paws the planks on the dock. He has mistaken my silence for assent. "Who but a misanthrope would live like this?"

"What's wrong with the way I live?" I ask a dog.

"What's wrong?" he says. "Where to begin? How many people watch *Murder She Wrote* reruns all day long? The show was bad enough the first time around. Now you watch the repeats, and the repeats of the repeats."

"Jessica Fletcher is an agent of justice. That is why I watch it."

"And why Junior Gilliam, whoever he may be?"

"Because he could turn a double play better than anyone in baseball. His pivot was poetry—*good* poetry. Not that you would appreciate such a thing."

"And why Blossom Dearie?"

"Because she sings on key, not that you . . ." I give him the first few bars of one of her blues standards: "Is you is or is you ain't my baby?"

"You live too much in the past."

"Where would you suggest I live?"

"In the moment!" he says, to my disgust. "You should be up on current events. You should watch *Press the Meat*." I would correct him, but I prefer his version. "And why aren't you writing something—I mean other than a lecture for the Chautauqua Institution about Lapham and the end of the world? Your last novel—when was it? Ten years ago?"

"Eight."

"And it was nuts. I should have seen all of this coming. A boxer who was so lovesick that he never ate or slept? Couldn't happen. Impossible."

"The boxer was a man."

"Oh. Well, I still think it was nuts. Who'd want to read such a thing?"

"No one, according to the sales reports."

"You need help."

"What else? What else is wrong with my life?"

"You mean apart from everything?" he asks. "You mean apart from your diet of ravioli, which you eat cold from the can, and Devil Dogs? Devil Dogs, indeed! There's a healthy food pyramid for you!"

I should explain that I eat things like Devil Dogs and cold ravioli because I have never learned to cook, though I used to be a master at takeout. I once received a call from a woman who was compiling a writer's cookbook—the favorite recipes of authors. I sent her four phone numbers.

"And your appearance! Everything you're wearing is ten years old."

"Not the bandage on my ear." He looks away. "And what about *your* appearance?"

"I'm perfect," he says. "I take care of myself." He curls up and licks his genitals, thinking that proves his case.

"And your computer," he goes on. "Why did you bother to get one? You only use it to communicate with your children, and to track your imagined archenemy, Mr. Lapham."

" 'Imagined'!" I lunge for him, but he skitters away.

"And then there's Chloe, seated forever at the kitchen table."

Perhaps I also should explain that the effigy of Chloe is a true work of art. The Hungarian dwarf in New Hampshire bridled when I asked him to put Chloe in shorts; he thought I was making fun of him. But temper aside, he has quite a good reputation. Not only is his work both accurate and imaginative; it is durable. When he finished the project, he told me, "This baby rules!" I resented the "baby" but was otherwise satisfied.

"And in the library," Hector continues. "One book. One book! In a writer's library! And what is that book? A slim volume of *The Vanity of Human Wishes*!"

"Because . . ." I start to say.

"Yes, yes. Because Dr. Johnson was always right. I don't know about that. I've never read him."

"You've never read anything," I remind him unkindly.

I suppose I ought to explain this as well, though why *The Vanity of Human Wishes* should require anyone's defense is beyond me. When my parents lived in this house, they packed the tall bookcases with the best that ere was thought or felt, as did the Marches before them. The books stretched from floor to ceiling, lined up in rows at the front of the shelves, like lewd and happy whores leaning on the windowsills of a Paris cathouse, their rosy tits spilling out of their housecoats, and calling to me: Come on up. So I did. Starting at the age of three, I climbed those shelves like a second-story man and sniffed and touched, and soon I could read. That continued until a few years ago—the reading, not the climbing.

But then one morning, not long after Chloe went west, I

regarded the high shelves with a new coolness approaching coldness, and I realized how much excessive activity was going on in those books as I stared at them. Hamlet whining, Anna moaning, Ahab yelling, the nitwit Daisy sobbing over shirts. The din began to get to me. Not that these characters hadn't a right to their tragedies and melodramas, but why did I have to be subjected to their squalid if well-wrought displays of passion? I had heard their stories once, and in most cases two or three times. Let them make their fusses elsewhere.

So little by little, I got rid of them by dumping them on the threshold of the Quogue Free Library, which, after all, is committed to preserving that clamor. I began with the most expendable: the complete James Whitcomb Riley, the too-complete Galsworthy, and Proust, who long had been getting on my nerves. Then I reached to pluck the higher orders of the likes of Swift, Mann, Eliot (George and T. S. both), Ellison, Dostoyevsky, Chekhov, Yeats, Márquez, Cavafy, Conrad, Baldwin, Malamud, Nabokov. Marianne Moore adjusted her tricorner and came along peaceably, as did Austen and Kafka, who said he had seen it coming. Chaucer chuckled. Emily Dickinson said she needed a change of scene anyway. But Twain, surprisingly, threw a hissy fit, and Joyce, as one might have expected, blew a gasket. Hemingway told me to go fuck myself. Off they went nonetheless, until there was but one work left on the shelves, right side, third shelf from the bottom, leaning casually against the wall—a single humble yet confident, self-aware yet not self-involved, brief yet eternally expansive book. This one I could not bring myself to toss. It made no unseemly noise. It did not plead for its life. It did not preen or strut. It was, in fact, the English language's supreme argument against noise, against pleading, preening, and strutting. See? Everything makes sense if you give it a chance.

"And while we're on the subject"—he never gives up—"what exactly is so great about Dr. Johnson? Everything you quote by him just sounds crabby to me, like someone else I know."

"Honor and principle, Mr. Tail. Honor and principle. Here's a story for you. While Dr. Johnson was working on his dictionary, which took him years and years, the Earl of Chesterfield, his so-called patron, was supposed to give him money to live on. But Lord Chesterfield never gave him a cent, with the result that Johnson was often at the point of starvation. When the dictionary was finished, however, and it began to be acknowledged as the monumental work of the age, Lord Chesterfield suddenly wanted to get in on the act and offered Dr. Johnson his help. Dr. Johnson wrote him the following: 'Is not a patron, my lord, one who looks with unconcern on a man struggling for life in the water and when he has reached the ground encumbers him with help?' Brilliant, no?"

He stares at me as though I were wearing a gorilla suit. "Do you realize you've told me that story a dozen times?"

"Yes. Yes, I do." I pat his head.

He sniffs, then snorts. "And look at your bedroom, which has nothing in it but a box spring and a mattress. And the parlor, which has no furniture at all. And the living room, in which you never set foot, with its tattered sofa—"

"It was *you* who scratched it to shreds, Mr. Tail."

"Sure, throw that in my face! I was just a puppy!" He shakes his fur into place. "Still, all of that would be excusable if you could not afford to live like a human being."

"Is that your standard?" I ask him. "Getting and spending? Yearning? You want a monument to yearning, like Lapham's over there?"

"But you're rich!" he says.

"I am *not* rich."

"You are! I've been in the Money Room."

He refers to a room in the house where I keep my fortune, whatever it amounts to, in stacks of cash bundled with paper bands. I refuse to use a bank not because I disapprove of banks but because I cannot abide talking about money, which is what they do in banks. My money comes from a couple of best-sellers I wrote many years ago. I have no idea how much of it there is, and I don't care. This drives Hector up the wall.

"Why don't we ever spend some of that money?" He is working himself into a rabieslike lather.

"On whom would I spend it?" I ask gaily.

"Well, you're going to lose it one day, mark my words." He paces, agitated. "A Money Room! You'll have a flood or a fire, and poof! All gone! You can take that to the bank."

"No, I can't."

"The point is, you spend too much time alone. All these crazy thoughts of yours come from living by yourself."

"I simply prefer solitude." Then, looking straight at him: "Though perhaps my life is not solitary *enough.*"

"You can't hurt me. I have God on my side."

"And if you want to know why I hate Lapham, it is precisely because he has attacked my solitude."

" 'I shall embrace mine enemy or I shall become mine enemy.' " He bites at the air.

"He has attacked my world, my middle-class, out-of-the-way, nonglittery, nontoxic yet occasionally useful world."

"So? He has his philosophy, you have yours. It's not personal."

"It's always personal, Mr. Tail. No matter what anyone tells you, all enmity is personal. And as much as I detest the ideological, mythical, symbolical, allegorical, abstractional Lapham for his grasping paws—you should pardon the expression—it is the noise he has brought into my head—*my* head, the head that belongs to me alone—that has shoved me over the edge. Look, do you think I would be preparing the Da Vinci, or even the Chautauqua lecture for that matter, were it not for Lapham? Do you?"

Of course he doesn't. I was a reasonably acceptable eccentric before Lapham banged into my life ten thrilling months ago. The essence of his crime against me is that he forced me to engage with the great wide world and, in so doing, to abandon my own. Worse, he forced me to do so *voluntarily*. Until he came into view and earshot, Noman was an independent country, existing modestly and decently apart from the great wide world of nations. Its insularity entailed the avoidance of alliances. It had an adequate if not a lavish economy, with a balanced budget and no national debt. It had its own customs, its own language, and its own rules and laws, which, though admittedly idiosyncratic, did not violate any international rules or laws. It had its own culture, such as it was, and its own animal life, such as he is.

But it had no armaments. Noman did not have armaments. And now, thanks to Lapham, it has been reduced to acting as any country would act, or react. Thanks to Lapham, Noman has become a nation like any other, just as predictable and armed to the teeth. That is the injury the Laphams of the great wide world inflict, you see. They make others as common as themselves. They bring you low. People see the House of Lapham, and they want one for themselves. Gaah. People watch Lapham make a public spectacle of himself, and they want to do the same. Modesty obliterated. Decency kaput. He who is inspired by envy inspires envy in others. Amen. On his way up, Lapham brings others down. And even those who oppose him, as I am about to do, are brought down as well, through their instruments of opposition.

"You make too much of Mr. Lapham," says Hector. "All he is doing is building a big house. Let him alone, and we'll be at peace again. Blessed are the peacemakers." I'd love to choke him. He goes on, "I really don't see what the big deal is. Isn't Mr. Lapham doing what everyone is supposed to do? Making something of himself?"

"He's making too much of himself," I tell him.

"But what's that to you?"

"You don't get this at all, do you? You think that Lapham's construction is limited to Lapham, or even to me and Lapham. Let me give you a lesson in the ripple effect. Already Lapham has invaded my mind. He has invaded Dave's mind, and Jack's and José's, and the minds of the Mexicans, even Kathy's—though that would be more like Germany invading Austria. Soon his monstrous house will have invaded the minds of all those who look upon it, and who comment upon it, and who write it up as the place to be for extravagant parties where birdbrains divine one another's chin tucks late into the night. The attendees at these parties will speak of them, and of Lapham, to others. His name will be synonymous with achievement and magnitude, and people will expect big things of him, as he will of himself. Eventually, everyone on the East End and beyond will be thinking of Lapham at the expense of everything of value. Soon all they will see is Lapham. He will have invaded the minds of the great wide world, as he has invaded my mind, as he has invaded Noman."

Hector shakes his head to suggest that I am a hopeless case, then walks away. I expected no better.

"Here's my point," I call after him. "My island sits in a creek, the creek opens to the canal, the canal opens to the bay, and the bay to the Atlantic. See what I mean?"

"Oh," he says without turning around. "*Our Town*—right? Loved it!"

Six

Hombres!" I raise my megaphone and shout to the Mexicans. "How much to stop work on Lapham's house?" It is high noon. They have been banging all morning.

They shout to me, "You don't have enough money, Señor March."

I shout to them: "How do you know?"

They shout to me: "Because we can see you!"

Everyone can see me; that's the trouble. This state of affairs did not exist before Lapham and his fellow vandals came to the shores across the creek. In those blissful days, there was no one to see me but the cormorants, the egrets, the moles, and the frogs. Now, not a week passes without some stranger's taking advantage of the sight of me by jumping into any available flotation device and cruising over for a chat. One thing to be said for living by yourself: no one can leave you. But people can visit.

In the past few weeks alone, I have suffered the forays of a string of uninvited guests. In dealing with such people, I have found that the straightforward approach works best, and so I try to be both forthright and as helpful as possible.

A delegation of Shinnecock Indians came over by canoe (as if that touch were necessary) to enlist my support for their plans to establish gambling casinos in Southampton. I gave it gladly. They were very grateful and made me an honorary member of the tribe. My Indian name is Walks Alone Awkwardly. They offered me twenty cartons of Marlboro Lights tax-free, but I declined. I asked if they realized that the land across the creek, on which the big houses are going up, had belonged to the Shinnecocks since 1561, or three hundred and thirty-three years before Southampton was incorporated. They said they were unaware of this. I assured them that the land was theirs and encouraged them to seize it at once. They said they would check their land records, which I knew would prove me right, since at one time or another the Shinnecocks have claimed every inch of the East End from Remsenberg to Montauk. We shook hands warmly and high-fived one another. Then they went home.

They were followed shortly afterward by the Southampton Hurricane of 1938 Society, a group devoted to commemorating everything connected with the hurricane of 1938, and to inserting mention of it in every possible conversation. They meet twice a week to recall the disastrous event, to look at faded black-and-white photographs of smashed boats and floating houses, and to lament that life in the Hamptons has gone "down, down, down" since those early days. They asked me if there might be some way to drive the Shinnecocks out of town, west toward Mastic and Bellport, or perhaps toward the northern jaw, whence they might paddle over the Sound to Connecticut and link up with their Pequot comrades in craps and blackjack. I told them I would give the matter serious thought and added that I was sure the Indians would not mind being expelled.

The Panel People (one man, one woman) from Panelle Hall in East Hampton came by to ask me to serve on a panel on the topic "Whither Literature?" I declined. How about a different panel, they asked: "Whither History?" The woman's hair was the color of bubble gum, and the man's eyelids covered most of his eyes, like the slats of a venetian blind. When I told them I didn't do panels, he said that gave him a brainstorm: how about a panel entitled "Panels: Good or Bad?" I showed them to their boat and said I'd get back to them.

A seventeen-foot Boston Whaler brought me a lanky, cactus-headed Amherst College English major on summer holiday with his parents in Wainscott. In his forties, he will stand before future students like an interminable book dog-eared to a meaningless page. He motored over to interview me for the honors thesis he is writing on my work. He told me my short stories have been anthologized for use in many colleges and universities. I asked him if any of those institutions were accredited. With specific regard to my work, he wanted to know if the presence of hats symbolized death. I told him yes. He asked if I deliberately avoided the gerund. I told him I did. He asked if I had been influenced by Salinger or by Eudora Welty. I told him yes, by both. He asked if he might send me his thesis when it was finished. I said, By all means.

"Are you going to read at the summer writers conference?" he asked, referring to a worthy event from which I long ago withdrew.

"No conferences, no seminars, no symposia, no colloquia, no festivals, no slams."

"Why don't you write anymore?"

"I forgot how," I told him, a little too close to the truth.

Two teenage girls from Westhampton High School, fair and skinny and both named Kristen, tied up at my dock but remained in their boat, and giggled. I asked them why they had come. They said they had heard I was a hermit, and they had never seen one before. I asked them what they thought a hermit looked like. They giggled some more. I brought them tall glasses of lemonade. They said thanks, giggled, and left.

Finally there was the FedEx man who delivered the Da Vinci parts, but unlike the others, he came at my insistence.

Initially, his company had rejected my shipment because it weighed three times the per-package limit of 150 pounds. But I found a way around that by requesting that it be delivered in three separate packages. This required the FedEx man to come over by barge on three separate occasions. By the last of these, he was sweaty and disgruntled. He dumped the parts on the dock. I caught him staring at the hole in my shirt. I'm sure he thought it was put there by a bullet. He told me that the next time I had a delivery weighing 435 pounds, I should try UPS.

He's had it in for me ever since he brought the current iteration of Chloe over on the barge several years ago. She weighed three pounds under the limit. I don't see what he was complaining about.

Of course, Dave the contractor comes over every so often to ask if I'm OK. I always tell him, "See for yourself."

With all this, it must be said that my visitors over these months, however noteworthy, did not compare either in number or in exotica to Lapham's. Mine were merely human. His consisted of objects and materials that were summoned to his ever-enlarging estate. Often I would sit on my dock and take account of them, make an actual list, I don't know why. But the arrivals constituted such a dazzling array—like foreign emissaries dispatched to state funerals—that, repelled as I was in principle, I nonetheless found myself gazing as would a child in a street crowd held back by police barricades as the inanimate celebrities made their appearances.

From Dorsetshire came fireplace stones that had been surgically removed from an English country manor built by Henry V for his fourth favorite mistress, Isabel of Rutherford. The gray stones had bloodred veins running through them, and were fabled to have turned this distinctive color when Henry had Isabel stoned to death after a drunken orgy, in which, incidentally, he had everyone stoned to death, including two royal macaws.

From Padua came hand-painted mantelpieces, twenty-four in all, each bearing stories of the Apostles, two mantelpieces for each, and stacked on the grounds like slices of toast. From Jerusalem, tiles inlaid with the faces of the Old Testament Prophets, to be used in Lapham's kitchen counters and on the backsplashes. From Oppressa, a small farming village outside Damascus, and known widely for its dancing calligraphers, came several precious tapestries with portions of the Koran woven in lavender. (Dave told me Lapham wanted all the major faiths represented in his home, and "a few minor ones.") From the Hopi came a fourteen-foot-high totem pole depicting various forms of foul weather. From the Pinga-poogoos, a tiny aboriginal sect that broke off from the main tribe in the 1960s, a stuffed kangaroo called Pek, the god of fertility and pugilism.

There was more: a solid piece of oak, oval in shape, fifty-six feet long, eleven feet at its widest, and honed from a single tree in the Black Forest, to be used as the dining room table (seats eighty comfortably). A bidet carved from a single piece of murky pink marble found only in a quarry in Oslo, by the hand of Carmen of Nordstrom. For the flooring in the upstairs hallway, a honey-stained maple discovered by Mrs. Lapham on a flying trip to Tblisi, a wood so strong and impermeable that Stalin had selected it for his casket and sepulcher. A spectacular front gate from the Tuxedo Park mansion of P. Lorilard, the drug manufacturer, which caught Lapham's eye because of the six-foot-high L centered in an iron parenthesis at the top, with molded bars of soap and toothpaste spilling from cornucopias on both sides.

Crockery from Delft; coffee mugs from Quito; theater seats rescued during the demolition of the old Palace on Broadway; and stadium seats from the Polo Grounds, to be set in tiers as grandstands for the grass tennis courts; three scatter rugs made from the hair of a dingo; a pair of combs from the tusks of a dugong; and a set of one-of-a-kind shaving brushes from the whiskers of a dikdik.

More still: maids' uniforms created in Nagasaki by seamstresses who were maimed but not incapacitated by the 1945 bombing, and which, according to Dave, gave Lapham the inspiration to order up his own underground bomb shelter on the property, for whose lining six tons of lead arrived in extra-wide loads from Des Plaines, Illinois. And green canopies for the beds from Uzbekistan in the guest rooms. And violet globes from Marseille for the reading lamps in the library, for which sixteen thousand volumes were purchased in bulk from used bookstores in Oxford (England and Mississippi) and Cambridge (England and Massachusetts). And, as of yesterday, painted panels of asparagus done by an artist in Winnipeg know for his renderings of vegetables. These, said Dave, will be hung on every wall of the house.

I don't know if he was pulling my leg, but Dave also told me that next week an artist from Albany will be arriving to paint the domed ceiling of Lapham's forty-seven-foot-high living room. Lapham said he wanted to provide a room that both creationists and those he called "evolutionaries" could feel comfortable in. So for his ceiling painting, he commissioned a depiction of Adam reaching out and extending the touch of life to a pollywog. I told Dave I could hardly wait to see the finished product, still thinking he was kidding. But he said, "Me too."

All such things, great and small, were delivered to the construction site by vans, station wagons, Jeeps, pickups, flatbeds, dump trucks, boats and helicopters, and deposited in their giant wooden crates on the grounds. I would sit and stare at them as, I imagine, the natives of Surinam, Jamaica, or of our own shores stared as warships, with bloated, bragging sails and teeming with strange men, entered the sky above the horizon and inched toward them, making not a sound and appearing out of nowhere, forever to ruin their lives. I stared as I am staring now, able to note my imminent destruction and unable to do a thing about it. That is, until today.

Suddenly I am aware of a difference in my atmosphere: the banging at Lapham's has stopped for an entire minute, a full sixty seconds. What has occurred, a peasant revolt? Have the overworked and underpaid Mexicans at last risen up against King Lapham the Striving? Have they tired of carting their tithes of chimichangas and quesadillas to their monarch's portcullis and decided to storm the castle instead, to stuff Lapham in a piñata and establish a utopian democracy in which all men and women of every race and nationality may live in peace and harmony, lacking neither black beans nor rice?

Has the mainland been hit by a thermonuclear device detonated by a maddened north-of-the-highway former dotcom millionaire who carried the bomb by hand in a Dean & DeLuca shopping bag and slipped it into the gigantic papier-mâché strawberry at the fruit and vegetable stand in Sagaponack? And yet if this is the case, surely the effects of the explosion, radiating from its strawberry epicenter, will reach as far as upstate New York. In which case, I don't think I shall sweat the Chautauqua lecture after all.

Silence. Even the caterwauling crows are hushed, taken aback by that noise which is the absence of noise. The air gulps. Then this: AAAAAAWWWWWWEEEEEE! Like a lion's roar amplified over a vast public-address system. A thousand times louder, a million. Never have I heard anything like it. It is as though the great mouth of the earth itself had opened to express the agony that the cauldrons of gravity were inflicting on it. It sounds like the word *awe:* AAAAAAWWWWWWEEEEEE.

My ears are screaming, including the one with the bandage. "José!" I yell. "Please stop that thing!" Hector is barking his head off. I wish.

Dave calls out, "I meant to warn you. Sorry."

"Sorry, señor," echoes José, sounding as if he meant it. The noise ceases for a second or two. "But we have to give it a test. Eees very special. Eees turbo. You know." It cries again: AAAAAWWWWWWEEEEEE.

"What is it?" I shout. At last they stifle the beast.

"Eees a Tilles, a Tilles Blowhard," says José. "The most powerful air conditioner ever built."

"A tea-less *what*?"

"Tilles," repeats Dave. They are passing the bullhorn back and forth. "Rhymes with *Phyllis*."

"Why does it need to be so loud?"

"Because eet not only cools the house," says José, "eet cools the whole property. Eees brand-new. Mr. Lapham has the first one in the whole wide world."

"What do you mean, it cools the whole property? It cools the air outside the house?" I strain to get a better look at the Tilles Blowhard, which is twice the size of my Da Vinci. It consists of an enormous potbelly with a curved smokestack whose opening is facing toward me, something like the Loch Ness monster in a ski mask.

Over the bullhorn, Dave explains that in an ordinary air conditioner, the fan motor and the blower feed the air through the coils of the condenser. But in a Tilles Blowhard, the fan motor operates at three hundred horsepower, and the blower is powered by a turbo engine that, if property angled, could fly of its own accord.

"Isn't that something!" Dave says. Jack nods rapidly. I cannot tell whether they are impressed or amused.

The grille, Dave goes on, has been replaced by an immense hornlike structure the size of a small cave. The thermostat is so sensitive that whenever the temperature in or around Lapham's house rises even one-tenth of a degree above the exquisitely calibrated ideal of sixty-five degrees Fahrenheit, the blower will pump a rainless hurricane of cold air through the great horn with such brutal force that anyone—say Lapham himself—who happened to be sitting in it at the time of the machine's eruption would be rocketed into the sky. Cherish the thought.

"All eight acres," says Dave. "It cools all eight acres. I've never seen anything like it."

José chimes in, "The whole enchilada."

"Did you really say that?" I ask him. He grins.

Perfect, is it not? The biggest house with the biggest everything, including a contraption that can alter the very air so it will conform to Lapham's standards and contribute to Lapham's comfort. How long before everyone out here wants a Tilles Blowhard of his very own? Can you not see it—all the emerald enclaves of the East End, one vast estate after the other, each securely equipped with the most powerful air conditioner ever built. On the patulous lawns, where once lolled Calders and Henry Moores, will squat the Blowhards. For who could be without one? Gaah. None of the denizens of Gin Lane in Southampton, certainly, or of Lake Agawam. Not a single home on Ocean Avenue in Bridgehampton, or on Sagg Main in Sagaponack, or on Lee Avenue or Lily Pond Lane in East Hampton, that's for sure. Nary a soul on newly rising Quogue Street, you can bet your bottom dollar. These estate sections that now gleam so demurely in the kingdom of the southern jaw, which already constitute the most desirable clusters of jewels in the most desirable universe, would never forfeit their chance to be cooler than ever.

The Tilles Corporation, Blowhard Division, will be hard pressed to meet the demand, but it rises to the challenge, because this phenomenon is no mere novelty, no fly-by-night cordless phone or waffle toaster or set of kitchen knives from Bavaria. The Blowhard represents a full-scale revolution in living. Soon it will be offered in colors: basic black—or Ice Ebony, if one is to be precise—will always remain a favorite, needless to say, but Frigid Aquamarine will put in a strong showing, as will Norse Coconut and Freeze Fuchsia. And Alaska Eggshell may one day turn out to be the most popular in the line. At parties, guests will survey their host's property and remark, "You've got the Eggshell. Lucky bastard."

But I know what you're thinking. What if all the Blowhards in all the estate sections in the Hamptons go off at the same time, and do it more than once a day, as is likely in late July, when the sun tends to make authoritative statements of its own? Will the decibel level—equivalent to that produced by ten thousand volcanoes erupting simultaneously—finally, when it blasts the buds from the bushes, shakes the ospreys from their nests, and geisers porgies and flounder out of the sea, be deemed too much to bear? Will the Blowhard (anti-ecology, "so yesterday") be discarded? Don't be silly. The proprietors will cope. They will wear earmuffs in July, in August even—whatever it takes. For the noise of the Blowhards will be a sign, like Edison's first incandescent lamps strung in an orange grove of lights along his New Jersey driveway, that the values of progress are in place and all is right with the world. Why, man, it will drown out the world's lesser, cheaper, more common noises! It will be *the* noise!

And dwelling thus in the bliss of a just-so temperature—even as the tumblers quake and tinkle, and the tea lights flicker and die—to whom will each and every Blowhard possessor trace his Fahrenheit Elysium? "You know, Lapham had the first one of these, the very first. You've met Lapham, haven't you? He has that super place in Quogue. A bit of a Blowhard himself—ha ha ha—but one hell of a guy!"

Dave, who is under the mistaken impression that I am more interested in cause than in effect, once again tries to explain to me exactly how revolutionary the Blowhard is. But I have already tuned him out.

"Do you get it now?" I ask Hector, who is still trembling from the AAAAAAWWWWWWEEEEE. "Self-consciousness leads to illegitimate superiority, which leads to materialism, recklessness, and the ruin of others."

"What?"

"Do I have to repeat myself?"

"Yes. My ears are a lot more sensitive than yours."

"Not since this morning." Against my better judgment, I take pity on him and ruffle the top of his head. "What I am telling you, my holy-rolling friend, is that the force that nearly deafened you just now is the force you should oppose. The Chautauquans want the twentieth century. Did you know that at the start of the twentieth century, ordinary people used to laugh at the self-aggrandizing antics of the big spenders? Cornelius Vanderbilt's re-creation of Versailles in Newport, and Potter Palmer, the Chicago store owner, loading down his wife with so many diamonds that she could barely stand upright. People once thought all that was funny. Today they envy what they laughed at.

"At the start of the twentieth century, one in every seven houses had a bathroom. A hundred years later, every seven bathrooms have a house." *Bang bang bang.* "Make that twenty bathrooms and two houses."

"You're just anticonservative," Hector says with a snort. "People in the Hamptons hate conservatives. But everyone will be conservative eventually, that's what I think."

"Don't waste that wisdom on me. Be a true evangelical: go door to door."

"In the same house?" He indicates ours.

"O Chautauquans," I cry out to no one in particular. "If only I could preach to you as though the Methodists were still in charge, and I were wearing a beard like the Smith

Brothers', and you were a tent community again, and we all lived in sepia tone. I would tell you to repent. I would urge you to acknowledge that your most valuable property is not real estate. It is *imagined* estate, which is not and has never been for sale."

"But why can't you have both?" asks Hector.

"Both what?"

"God and mammal."

"Mammon."

"Whatever. Why can't you have riches on earth and riches in Paradise? I say aim for the skies!"

"That's the plan, my boy."

José calls across the creek to ask if I would care to hear the Blowhard again. *"No más,"* I plead, raising my hand in a Roberto Duran surrender.

"You should get one of these things yourself, Señor March—if you can afford it, wheech I theenk you cannot. But if you could, you would never again be hot in the summer."

"That would be heaven," I tell him. I am encouraged to see that he, Jack, and Dave are all laughing.

Seven

Have I mentioned that I communicate with Lapham? I have no direct dealings with him, but I do correspond with his executive secretary or manservant or amanuensis or creepy-crawly or whatever he is called. A certain Damenial Krento. I send my notes to Lapham by boat across the creek. Not by my real boat, one of the row-row-row variety that I keep tied to the dock inside the *L*, to protect it. For Krento I bought a fiberglass toy motorboat, battery-powered, cerulean blue, with black-and-silver warheads decaled on the sides, about two and a half feet in length and one foot wide. It is quite sturdy. It does not capsize. I skew it toward the current at an angle upstream (tides and currents are treacherous in the creek), and I keep it on course using a remote control. I have named the boat *Sharon*, a female version of Charon, the grizzly old sailor of Greek mythology who ferried the dead across the river Styx in the Underworld.

I tuck my message into *Sharon*'s tiny cabin, guide the craft carefully, watch it make landfall, and wait for a reply.

I send the same note every day: "Mr. Lapham, tear down that house!" I thought that the Reaganesque echo might appeal to him.

As of 1:06, I have received no response to today's note. When Krento is ready, he signals me with a huge red-white-and-blue yachting flag, and I switch on the remote. Because he is apparently on the short side and also somehow translucent, the flag often looks as if it were waving itself. But his reply, too, is always the same: "Dear Mr. March: Mr. Lapham is in receipt of your recent letter. He takes this opportunity to express his gratitude to you for taking the time to write to him. That is why he is writing to you. He wishes you continued success in your endeavors. Yours very sincerely, Damenial Krento, executive secretary to Mr. Lapham."

Once, in a faint attempt at sabotage, I wrote to Krento himself and asked if he would like to quit Lapham's employ and come work for me instead. I had never had an executive secretary before, I told him, but I was sure I could find several secretaries for him to execute. I could not pay what Lapham did, alas, but I could promise him the use of one excellent book that he might pick up and put down again as many times as he liked, as well as the best Devil Dogs and cold ravioli he had ever tasted in his life. He wrote back that he was grateful for my correspondence, and he also thanked me for it.

Bark bark bark bark bark. Hector goes off like a burp gun, eyes glazed in full dogdom. *Bark bark bark.* I yell at him to stop. Now the Mexicans join in, *con gusto. Bang bang bang bang bang. Bang bang bang. Bark bark bark.* There is nothing I can do about the Mexicans, but Hector?

"Could you possibly be any *less* cooperative?" I ask him.

He squares around to confront me. "Perhaps if you had sent me to business school, as I asked you to, and more than once, a lot more, I might have picked up some people skills."

At one point he wanted to go to the Harvard Business School. Setting aside the practical difficulties of enrolling a dog in any educational establishment other than obedience school (which in his case would have been a joke), I tried to explain to him that all he would learn there was bottom-line thinking, rapaciousness, and corporate crime.

"I don't mind learning those things," he said. "I'm not like you. I want to make something of myself." Then he licked his nose.

"I can teach you all you need to know right here."

"I don't believe in homeschooling," he said. "Except for Bible classes."

"Well, you're not going to the Harvard Business School. You probably couldn't get in, and in any case, it's too expensive."

"Very nice. Treat me like a dog, why don't you?"

"You *are* a dog."

"Well, then!" And with that, he proceeded to bark all night, as he is barking now.

A wind moves across the island like the dismissive or blessing gesture of a hand, and then is gone. One learns to appreciate the wind in later life, after all the sunsets have been oohed to death, and the sunrises greeted with stupendous boredom, and the size of the oceans commented upon ad infinitum, not forgetting the frothy whitecaps and the ever-receding horizon, and the moonlight too, of course, which is alternately sexy and melancholy, and the chirpings of birds, which are alternately sweet and delphic—after all the appropriate metaphors and similes have been delivered unto every eclectic feat or whim of nature, one wakes up to the quality of the wind, the beauty of which is that it is noticed only when it touches something else.

The dog, he barks. The House of Lapham, she bangs. Tempus fugit. Carpe diem. Cave canem. The clouds form Rorschach inkblots, which look to me like a row of cannon in a field.

What shall I wear for you, dear Chautauquans? I have too

many outfits to choose from: the blue blazer, white shirt, and charcoal-gray slacks ensemble; the blue blazer, white shirt, and medium-gray slacks ensemble; the blue blazer, white shirt, and light-gray slacks ensemble. I lay out the combination with the charcoal slacks, having discovered large holes in one of the two remaining pairs, and the crotch nearly vanished from the other. A few sorry threads stretch across the breach, like bamboo bridges in World War II.

It is of no importance. I realize that if all goes as it should tonight, this may be my last day on Noman, at least until I am released from custody.

"Good-bye, Blossom. Good-bye, Junior." I stride through my house bidding personalized farewells to the furniture, the appliances, and the utensils. And I bestow an affectionate au revoir on Chloe, who appears unmoved.

"Why aren't you saying good-bye to me?" asks Hector.

"Because you're coming with me. We've been through all this before."

"*You've* been through all this. Don't I have rights?"

"No," I tell him. "But if you're a good dog, I will let you give the lecture for me, from the West Highland perspective."

I pause in my library to pay homage to Dr. Johnson with a respectful nod. Then, for the first time in weeks, I notice my computer screen. I have old e-mails from the children.

Dear Dad:

Mom says you're going nuts—something about someone building a house. Don't worry. You can always live with us, in the basement.

Love,

Charles

Dear Dad:

Mom says you're going ape—what's new? Don't worry. You can always live with us. We have a cage.

Love,

Emma

Dear Dad:

Mom says you're going postal. Don't worry. You can always live with Charles or Emma.

Love,

James

Incautiously, I now recognize, I e-mailed Chloe when Lapham first started banging, to ask if she recalled where I kept the flamethrower. I had better respond to the children at once.

Dear progeny:

Thank you for your messages. I can assure you that there is no cause for alarm. Please calm your mother as well, if that is possible. As to the matter of her concern, I am coming to the end of a great new undertaking that not only will gratify me personally but, if viewed in the proper light, also will save much of civilization, now and for years to come.

Love,

Dad

There. That should allay everyone's fears.

As long as I'm at the computer, I take the opportunity to "visit" Lapham's Web site. The banner headline announces: *Lapham Considers Senate Race.* I have no way of knowing whether this represents authentic news or whether it is simply one of the daily flailings of his mind. In another, earlier memo to his public, he announced that he was thinking of buying the Time Warner Company, but he soon learned that it was not for sale, for once. Some years ago, he briefly did produce his own magazine, which he called *Lapham's Weekly.* Its chances of success were impaired by his refusal to hire an advertising director, mistakenly assuming that old family friends could be counted upon to take out ads, just as they might in a high-school yearbook; he insisted on writing all the articles himself; and it came out monthly.

The current bulletin continues: "Fed up with politics as usual," Lapham says he is "chucking his hat" into next year's "Senate ring." He has concluded that the "times call for an independent thinker" like himself, someone who will not "be beholden to special interesting groups." What this country needs is "new beginnings." He "believes in America." He confesses to being a "hapless romantic." Soon, he promises, he will be sending out a series of "boardsides" on public policy issues. "More to come." Not if I can help it.

He elaborates upon his senatorial ambitions. He sets out his positions on such matters as abortion, which he is "neither for nor against," and school prayer, which he suggests "requires future study." He is for equal opportunity but against quotas; he thinks that affirmative action "is a fine idea but should be controlled." He supports public schools, yet "nothing beats a good prep-school education." He will continue to fight for the separation of "church and statehood," though for his own part, he always will do "what the good Lord says." I should get Hector to ask the good Lord if Lapham is also considering running for the presidency.

There are several attachments and appendices. The first of these is the text of a speech that Lapham delivered to the members of the Yale Club of Schenectady, in which he praised the "incomparable value" of legacies. I'll bet.

Next is a transcript of a speech he gave at the Devon Yacht Club of East Hampton, concerning the incomparable value of the coat-and-tie rule. In Lapham's view, eliminating this tradition, as some of the club's "younger scamps" had proposed, would be "paramount" to striking at the club's heart, though he allowed as how he'd been young once himself and well recalled how "darned uncomfortable" those neckties could get on an August night.

And then there is a sampling of the candidate's "fugitive thoughts" on various issues. On the economy: "Business is good for business." On gay and lesbian marriage: "I think it should be left up to the cities." On jobs: "The more jobs, the better." On immigration: "If foreign people will work for less pay, fine. But they should not drive out real American workers." I think I'll print out that one for the Mexicans.

On war:

I do not believe that Americans should send our young people into harm's way where they might lose life and limb unless the war is in America's best interests. For example, if some country somewhere is having a civil war, I say that's OK as long as it doesn't get out of hand. If England or Russia or some European country had interfered with *our*

Civil War, where do you think we would be now? On the other hand, if the American man, woman, or child is going to suffer because some other country attacks us or has something we need, then I declare: Bring it on!

I wish I could say it was inconceivable that a man like Lapham could gain public office. But look who holds public office now. The times call for a man who believes in nothing. He runs because he knows the people expect him to believe in nothing, and *want* him to believe in nothing, because they too believe in nothing. Thus he becomes a man of the people. Nothing comes of nothing.

Say, do you think I would make a good King Lear? Gold pointy crown? White flowing beard and robes? There's no heath on my island, but I could be holding a Heath Bar. Tell me. Don't hold back. *Bang bang bang bang bang.*

"There's no doubt about it now," I tell Hector. "No question as to my course of action now."

"Really?" He yawns, his jaws gaping like a crater.

"Yes. No question at all. You know, Hector, it occurs to me that this may be the most important day of my life, the moment when all the stray and whorling strands of my existence merge into one clear, straight ribbon of light, and I at last win the towering moral satisfaction due all those who are driven to defend what is decent, modest, and right in the world."

He looks up devotedly. "Then again, you may be ready for a straitjacket."

Yes, by all means run for the Senate, Lapham, old boy. And after that, who knows? Perhaps the country cottage you are building across the creek from me will one day become the nation's next Hyannisport or Kennebunkport or Key Biscayne or Crawford. How lucky I will be to live so close to the President's summer White House. The dignitaries who will come for visits. Foreign ministers. Supreme Court justices. Country-and-western singers. Astronauts. The Bassoonist Marching Band from Little Rock. The national champion cow tipper from Omaha. The Secret Service agents with their trousers rolled, carrying Uzis and patrolling the creek in narrow-eyed vigilance. To think: a poor boy like myself, a humble artist with no claim to noble lineage, hanging out my shingle so near the home of the leader of the free world. How should I put it? A stone's throw?

Eight

"Why do people give lectures?"

"To hear themselves talk."

"Is that why you're doing it?"

"No. I'm providing an indispensable lesson."

"Oh, yes. I forgot."

"Because ideas matter, Mr. Tail."

"*Your* ideas."

If only the construction of the lecture gave me as much pleasure as that of the Da Vinci. Words: I still believe in them. I do. It's in my blood. Yet I could present the Chautauquans with whole pyramids of words, the Great Pyramid itself, cladded with words on the outside, and words within, and detailing the entire disastrous course of the twentieth century from Sarajevo to Sarajevo, and the immense edifice would not hold a candle to some gizmo thought up thousands of years ago by illiterates without indoor plumbing or spandex. Under the black tarp stands a monument to form and function, though it also calls forth individual interpretation. From the front, it looks like a skier holding tall, thick poles, staunch and symmetrical. From the side, it resembles a rudimentary car. From above, it's a funeral bier with the body laid out in the shape of a cross. From behind, a vertical snake seen from the back, peering over a fence.

How did they do it, those savage geniuses? Why did they do it? Because they knew they had to survive in a dangerous and threatening world. Naked and exposed though they might be, they had to fight back. And though they could not see beyond their noses, they peered into the future as well. Without realizing it, they dreamed of Lapham.

Two P.M. Odd that I still have not heard from him. Perhaps he has finally tired of my one-line notes and has instructed Krento not to reply. Should I send him a more ample communication?

"What do you think of this?" I ask Hector, wishing I had someone else to consult.

Dear Lapham,

Once again this morning I was awakened by the noise of your erection. Have you no shame? Do you know what a house is? A house is a place where the mind finds its outer shape, its carapace. It should be a work of sculpture, of ceramics, fired from within. A house has a purpose, a significant purpose, as a person must have a purpose. A house is a protection, a solace, a thought. It is not a dick, Lapham. Not an organ perpetually driven by modern pharmaceutical stimulants to grow like Jack's beanstalk until it punctures heaven itself. Neither should it stand as a temple to individual glory. Even Gatsby's house was not that. Somewhere in that musty family history of yours, down the lightless arched corridors of framed portraits of deposed Laphams, including Moses, the founder of the asparagus feast, there must be a reference to decency, to manners. Look it up, Lapham. Learn something for a change. Tear down that monument to the national boast. Put up a log cabin in its place and live out your days in solitude, gratified by the accomplishment of good works. Will you do that, Lapham? Or will you build and build until the entire East End is your personal property, a gated fortress starting at the Suffolk County line? Lapham, you yourself are hell. I loathe and despise you.

Yours sincerely,

Harry March

"Irresistible," says Hector. He walks off hurriedly, as if he has suddenly remembered an assignment.

Where is Lapham holed up, I wonder, as he awaits the completion of his monstrosity? Living in another monstrosity, I have no doubt, some barely adequate twenty-thousand-square-foot shack that he has rented for the duration at a price that would feed New York's homeless for three months. How bravely he endures the wait. I cannot picture him; I never have been able to. I envision only his head in shadow, very large, like a bobble head, and his voice like a limp stocking hanging over the rim of a sink.

Ah. No sooner does this feckless musing pass than what do I spy but Krento signaling me to use the remote. *Sharon* is putting toward me from across the sea. Assuming that she contains Krento's usual reply, I am about to toss away the letter when something catches my eye: the signature is still in Krento's fine, smarmy hand, but the text is unusually long.

What will you be telling me, Mr. Lapham? What curses will you hurl, what outrage will you reluctantly express? How much patience do you have left, or have you perhaps run out? To what branch of the authorities will you report me? The local police? The FBI? The ASPCA? Or have you instead handed over the matter of my hostile correspondence to your team of buttoned-up family lawyers-in-waiting, Arthur, Carther, and MacArthur? Are you threatening to sue? Or will your public-relations people pillory me in pamphlets? Do you have connections to the mob? Will I end up swimming in the creek with the other poor fishes?

I take my time opening the note. This is momentous, is it

not? It is the closest I have come to him yet. I am Holmes, finally confronting Moriarty. Let it fly, Lapham. Do your worst.

The letter:

Mr. Lapham has instructed me to inquire if you would be available on the thirteenth of September next for a dinner at his new residence, across the creek from your own. Mr. Lapham knows you have taken an interest in this, his latest domicile, which, we are very pleased to say, will be complete and ready for entertaining on the above date. He would be quite pleased if you would join a few selected guests who are to dine with him and Mrs. Lapham that evening to celebrate the auspicious event. Could you let us know at your earliest convenience whether you will be able to attend?

With highest regards,

Yours sincerely,

Damenial Krento

Whenever things like this happen to me, I wonder what unforgivable crimes I must have committed in previous lives. Ordinarily I do not believe in the phenomenon of previous lives (for me, one life has been plenty), but no other explanation will do. At such times I try to recapture a past existence, to look into the eyes of the sweet pink babies of Alexandria as I prepared to slaughter them with my battle-ax; to behold the quavering nuns in a French convent in Nigeria shortly before I went on a spree of rape and decapitation; to gaze over a field of a million Chinese peasants, lying supine in the sorghum, immediately following my machete jubilee and just before I set fire to the bodies.

Only such savageries and worse could possibly account for the punishment I face in my current life: having to sit down at the Laphams' fifty-six-foot dinner table honed from the Black Forest and be forced to speak of the latest article on Canadian utility rates in *Farquar* magazine and the latest exhibit at the Krapp. Only the most extravagant acts of past-life murder and evisceration could justify my having to turn to my left and right to exchange chitchat about the best Pilates class on the planet or the best flat-screen TV on the planet, or the best dry cleaner, gelato-maker, gnocchi, blogger, or the best grout on the planet; and Isn't she awful, and Isn't he horrible, and Don't they both look fantastic; or having to crane my neck toward the extreme ends of the table in order to fling compliments on the cold leek soup, which is also the best on the planet, and to which I'd like to raise a glass, as I would to the Laphams in their hosty glory: "Running for the Senate, are we, Lapham? Good show!"

I try not to dwell on the buried insults in Krento's note— the question of my availability for the dinner party and the reference to my "interest" in Lapham's house. Far more pressing, and more alarming, is the announcement that the "residence" will be finished in something less than six weeks. Even as I hold the note in my hand, growling trucks are delivering slabs of sod to Lapham's property: a ready-made lawn, to be laid much as a carpet is laid. Dave's assurances aside, I have had no idea how close the "domicile" is to completion. I glance at the brooding bulk of the tarp and congratulate myself on my sense of timing.

"Dear Mr. Krento." Rather than excuse my absence with the heartbreaking account of my recurring case of rickets, I decide to reply in kind.

> I am in receipt of Mr. Lapham's gracious invitation, and it is with the greatest pleasure, and honour, that I accept. I was wondering, Mr. Krento, if it would be proper for me to bring my own wine. Of course, I would share it with the Laphams and the other guests.
>
> Yours sincerely,
> Harry March

By return boat comes Krento's answer:

> Mr. Lapham will be delighted to learn that you will be in attendance at his dinner party on the thirteenth of September next. There is no need to bring your own wine, unless,

of course, you prefer to. Mr. Lapham's forty-six-hundred-square-foot wine cellar, the largest of its kind in North America, boasts the finest French, Italian, Australian, Californian, and North Fork wines in the world. On the evening in question, he will be serving several choice vintages of Vosne-Romanée. I trust you will enjoy them.

Back goes *Sharon:*

Very pleased to learn that good wines will be served. I had intended to bring a case of Château Petrus, 1961, but am content to leave it at home. By the by, will you be serving asparagus? I am uncertain as to the proper way to eat it.

I am also concerned about the dress code. Should I wear a necktie, and if so, should it be of the bow persuasion or a four-in-hand? Should I wear a colorful sweater, something pink or light orange perhaps, and ought I to put it on or drape it over my shoulders in that rakish way that men in summer do? Should I wear Louis Vuitton loafers? If so, with or without socks? What about slacks? Should I wear them? Plaid or white or golf-course green? If I wear a polo shirt, should the collar be turned up or down? An ascot? Or is that over the top? Should I wear anything over the top?

Yrs. sincerely

The wait for a reply is longer this time. I suspect that Krento is confused by my tone and has chosen to confer with a fellow assistant or with Lapham himself. Twenty minutes later, give or take, my ship comes in.

Dear Mr. March:

Mr. Lapham has passed along the following communication: "Please tell him to be as comfortable as he wishes. We don't stand on ceremony in the Lapham household."

That I believe. I write back:

Mr. Krento:

Would you be kind enough to let me know what my conversation ought to consist of at Mr. Lapham's dinner party? I enclose a list of possibly suitable topics that you must feel free to edit. They are as follows: The absolutely terrifying piece on soccer moms in Mozambique in the *Financial Times*. The absolutely hilarious column on animal names in the *Wall Street Journal*. The absolutely scary economy. The absolutely hopeless Mets. The absolutely porous ozone layer. The absolutely fabulous Tiger.

Other things I might wish to say: "I thought life was supposed to slow down the older you got!" "Where did the summer go!" "Being a grandparent is just the best!" And

"Hey!" And "Hi!" And *There* he is." And *There* she is." I would like to say those a lot. And "Great!" I should like to say that as well.

And may I pose a question for all the guests to respond to one by one at the dinner table? Something about the future of the Democratic Party? I love it when they do that during meals. And may I cite someone in the news and offer an astoundingly clever interpretation of his or her actions, something fresh, possibly risqué, something no one else has thought to say? May I do that? Please advise.

Krento's reply:

Mr. Lapham says anything you would care to say will be most welcome. He adds that you exhibit signs of a delightful sense of humor. May I say I concur wholeheartedly?

You may, Krento, old bean. You may. I steer *Sharon* back with a final note of thanks, happy in the knowledge that the question of my accepting any invitation at all from the House of Lapham will soon be moot.

Nine

Lest you conclude that my aversion to social events derives solely from my odd cast of mind, or assume that it is simply an invention to bolster a cute curmudgeonliness, having no foundation in real experience, I should like to describe the last Hamptons dinner party I went to, about eight years ago.

Chloe and I still were together then. She had accepted an invitation from a couple of middle-aged writers who were so embittered by the success and/or happiness of others that they had both shrunk to the size of lizards and were heading in the direction of total disappearance, though not quickly enough to prevent their intrusion into my life. When I complained to Chloe about being forced to show up at their annual summer paella and beef tournedos fiesta—or, as they called it, their surf-and-turf orgy—she smiled her who-cares smile and patted my head, at which she then hurled that vilest of commands: *Mingle*.

"*No*, you don't have the vapors. No one these days has the vapors. We're going. That's that. And just once, please don't play the cigar-store Indian. Most of these people are perfectly nice. If you spent half as much time talking to human beings as you do to that dog, these things wouldn't get under your skin."

The Bittermans' house in Sagaponack stood back from a road near the beach, behind a tangle of shrubs and mounds of grassy sand. It was built in the early 1800s, during the Jackson administration, and was purchased in the 1970s for a song—one that the couple sang frequently and without prompting. It featured wide-board floors, exposed beams, bullet-glass windows, wainscoting, and all the other stations of Kathy Polite's cross. Except for the residents, on whom it was wasted, it was just the sort of home one might wish for, and not too different from my own, save for the fact that my house was intended for living in, and theirs for the approval of others.

When we pulled up (in Chloe's car; I never wanted one), I spotted Jack, Dave's boy, who was working as one of the valet parkers, even though he was way underage.

"*The Rocky Horror Show*?" I asked him.

"*The Night of the Living Dead*," he said, taking my keys.

"Wanna switch places?" I offered. He drove off smiling. Chloe scowled.

Down a sinuous flagstone pathway, under a trellis of white roses, into a garden necklaced with Japanese lanterns, green and tangerine, and there we were. Before us stood the lowing herd who have populated one another's parties in alternating states of espièglerie and gloom every summer, summer after summer, for twenty or thirty years. As we entered, several of them shot me glances of acknowledgment and contempt, my usual greeting. One especially hate-filled look came from a woman who had stopped speaking to me years earlier, after I reluctantly participated in one of her famous word-game soirées. She had asked her guests to respond reflexively to a series of questions; we were to identify, in turn, our favorite city, U.S. President, ocean, food, and animal. My choices were Perth Amboy, Harding, the Arctic, redheads, and the mosquito.

Whenever I approach any gathering of people, I do so self-numbed, the way I imagine Greek infantrymen must have hurtled across blackened fields toward their enemy and certain death: my chest exposed, my eyes the whites of hard-boiled eggs.

But Chloe breezed among the guests like a love song, cursed as she was with the embracing nature of Browning's last duchess. Luckily for her, I was no duke. I watched her weave and dance from cluster to cluster, glanced up at the sweet velour of a Hamptons sky, and checked the time.

For a year or two I stood there in my wretched awkwardness, searching in vain for the arrival of a street gang from Chinatown or a shipment of curare. Instead I was approached by a houseguest of the Bittermans', a man my own age with dark, thick eyelashes like the prongs of a rake. He introduced himself as Jeff Jefferson, a vintner from Cutchogue, on the island's northern jaw. He had provisioned the party with cases of a new Margaux, which he said had no taste, though he was "going to promote the hell out of it" anyway. Why did he strike up a conversation with me? Because his new wife was getting started as a writer, and he thought perhaps I might give her some tips.

He pointed her out across the lawn. She was a hard-looking blonde, deep into her twenties, wearing an ooh-la-la floral dress with gardenias at the breasts. I repeated my standard response for such situations.

"Just urge her to keep at it," I said heartily, meaning the opposite.

"That's great advice." He thumped me on the back and tried to catch his child bride's attention so he could summon her to where we were standing. But I pretended that I wanted to go speak with Vandersnook. "Later, then?" he asked. I nodded.

Vandersnook was a once-able writer who now lived off

large lecture fees and a rugulose puss that looked like its own caricature. So distinctive and adorable was his face, in fact, that it appeared in ads for bookstores all over the country. He had written two good novels long ago, but then he had become himself. His recent refusal to read from his work at the White House would have been more impressive had he been asked.

"Well, well! What have we here? Harry March, the man who wasn't there."

"And Vandersnook, the man who is always here," I replied, at his level of wit.

"We're mounting a campaign that I'd like to enlist you in," he said. He did not wait for my what-is-it because he knew it would never come. "The summer writers conference is using the big conglomerates to sell the authors' books. They're snubbing our local bookstores. It's a disgrace."

"A crime against humanity," I agreed. "But isn't the conference run on a shoestring?"

"I'll say! I told them I'd give a reading this summer, but when I found out what they'd pay, I bowed out."

"So you're campaigning against them because they can't pay your fee?"

"It's the only right thing to do. Who else is going to help the little guy?" He studied his wineglass. "By the way, don't drink the Margaux. It's shit."

Just then my shoulder was tapped by a woman who simply

presented herself. She smiled expectantly, baring teeth even whiter than Kathy Polite's in a face like a pink sponge. She came up to my chest. I thought she might be a cake.

"Remember me?" My blankness betrayed me. "You don't, do you?" I was relieved to realize that she thought she had changed so much, and for the better, as to be revealing to me some biological transformation.

"You look so different," I said.

"Can you believe it?"

"I can't."

"Isn't it wonderful what they can do these days!" All her parts giggled, including the new ones.

"You can say that again."

"Well, it's certainly great to see you. Would you like my phone number?" she asked.

"No thanks. I might lose it."

To give you an idea of how the rest of the party went, that was by far my most cordial and instructive conversation of the evening.

The male Bitterman called everyone to dinner. For a brief moment I malingered and relished the sight of my fellow guests' backs. In the distance I heard the moaning of a train, mixing urgency with melancholy and eternal escape.

"Surf and turf, everybody!" Mrs. Bitterman urged, followed by the raucous laughter of all.

In the public room where we were to dine, whiteness was everywhere: the tablecloths, the linen napkins, the candles, the flowers, the frocks of the ladies, their blouses of silk, the slacks of the men, and their billowy shirts. In the corners of the room were chairs and ottomans upholstered in white duck, white wicker stools, and a chalky sectional beneath a painting of a sailboat, white, in a white frame. Against the white walls stood white bookshelves, containing books with white bindings.

Most of the observable skin was white as well, a consequence of cancer research and precautions. But some few heliotropes had taken the reckless road into the sun and were all the more interesting as a result, not only for the maplike stains on their faces and the dark creases like narrow streets to unknown destinations, but also for the oh-to-hell-with-it attitude that had created those stains and creases in the first place. Browned and gleaming, they were talking cadavers, the comedy of their outsides doing battle with the tragedy of their insides. I could not help but admire them.

The room held six round tables each set for eight, with names written out by hand on place cards bearing an embossment of tiny pink seashells. As always, the seating assignments had their categorical logic. There was the table for the politicians, among them the Politician of the Hour, a senator or cabinet member who during the previous week had done something heroic, stupid, unethical, or criminal (it did not matter which). There was the table for the journalists. They used to separate TV journalists from print journalists, but that practice ended once there was no difference between them. There was the table for members of the Council on Foreign Relations, who were placed together so that they could agree with one another, but with just one cavil and two demurrers. There was the table for the Perfects, whose number this night included one of our hosts (the other joined the journalists) and, of course, Chloe. And finally there was the Misfit Table, customarily populated by one aggressive psychiatrist, one Englishman who just loved everything about America, one woman with a cause, one agreeable person (generally a man), a pill (a man or a woman), two surprised people who said nothing (a man and a woman), each bearing the look of someone who had been sitting in the whistle of a steamship when it went off, and me.

Fate saw to it that I was seated between the woman with the cause and the pill (female). The first, on my left, addressed me at once. "I do hope you're doing something for the wheels," she said. She was a handsome old bat, with eyes like coagulated sapphires, and a face wrapped tight about the skull. Her stare was so penetrating, I thought she was blind.

"Something for the wheels?" I asked.

"Yes. They're in very bad shape. A man in your position could do a great deal for them."

"What trouble are the wheels in?"

"Dire. Dire," she said. "In fifty years, perhaps less, there will be no wheels left. What do you think of that?"

"I think the world will be stationary."

"Well! That doesn't make any sense whatever. Either take the problem seriously, or not at all!" The agreeable man concurred with her. The surprised people were surprised.

"And what do you do?" asked the pill to my right. She looked like the second Mrs. Humbert Humbert, lurid and nuts, with the sort of poise that readily transmogrifies into belligerence. I pictured pink cozies on her toilets. When she spoke, she bobbed and weaved like a bantamweight.

"I'm a writer," I answered.

"Would I have read anything you've written?"

"That depends. I'd have to have some idea of what you read."

"Well, I may have read something you wrote without knowing you wrote it."

"That's sensible but unhelpful," I said, "since I still have no way of knowing your reading habits."

"I was only trying to make pleasant conversation." She spun huffily toward the Englishman, who said something about how exciting it was to hear Americans quarrel, because we're so free.

A sputter of shouting outside distracted me from the festivities. I heard someone yelling at Jack to hurry up and park his car already because he was late to the dinner. For his part, Jack was explaining as courteously as he could that the cars had to be moved in order of their arrival. But the guest was late, after all, so he had to take it out on a thirteen-year-old boy.

Just then, from the other side of the table, the psychiatrist said to me, "I know you. You wrote that novel about the man who hid out and lived in a rare-book store." He had the pasty, piggy face of a Williams graduate I once met in the 1960s, and he scrutinized my being as if he had just picked me out of a police lineup. "I hope you don't mind my saying so, but I thought it was silly."

"Why would I mind a thing like that?"

"I mean, it was unrealistic. How could someone live in a bookstore without being caught?"

"It was supposed to be metaphorical," I said. I don't know why.

"Metaphorical for what?"

"For a mind that wanted to live in the past."

"There you go," he announced to the entire table. "Silly."

"Maybe you'll like my new novel better," I suggested. "It's about a fat, pale Williams graduate who eats tapioca for a year until he explodes."

"Are you being funny?" Pasty was turning maroon.

"Not in the least. And the story is *not* metaphorical either. It really happened. Or soon will."

Before he could say anything else, Mrs. Bitterman stood and clinked her Waterford crystal goblet with her demitasse spoon. "It's so nice to have all our crowd together under one roof," she said. "As Yeats wrote, '. . . that I had such friends.' Now I should like to propose a toast to my fabulously talented husband, who has just finished his book on the life of Louella Parsons. It's called *Poop*. And I will tell you, it is absolutely fabulous!" Mr. Bitterman waved off the prearranged flattery from his seat. The applause crinkled like cellophane.

The news of Bitterman's achievement had hardly settled over the tingly room when a woman at another table stood and clinked her glass. This one had always interested me. Naturally gifted in malice and deceit, she never had to choose between betraying her friends and betraying her country. She had an announcement to make, about herself: "Yes, I know. You were wondering, 'Will she ever get it done?' The answer is a resounding *yes*, as of three o'clock this afternoon! At three o'clock today, *Winner: The History of the Pulitzer Prizes*

hopped from my screen to my printer and thence to the publisher!" Cries of "Oh!" competed with cries of "Hurray!,"
with cries of "Hurray!" coming out on top.

As if all this were not enough to hurl "our crowd" into a
never-ending saturnalia, a magazine writer and his wife then
shot to their four feet to say that they too had finished not one
but two books that very day. Their faces, a pair of andirons,
were softened by the couple's identical robin's-egg-blue
seersucker jackets. Each had written a biography of the other,
and the volumes were to be released as a twinned, boxed pair
titled *He Writes* and *She Writes*.

"That is fantastic!"

"Marvelous!"

"Brilliant!"

"Hurray!"

"Hear! Hear!" from the Englishman.

Dickie Weeke, "the adman with clout," a galoot with a
mind like a dead battery, went so far as to say he intended to
buy a hundred copies of the set's first printing. Chip (Chip)
Cheroo, the cultural critic whose ingenuity in the torture of
prose was not to be laughed at, thundered "Ditto!" And Bobo
de Pleasure, the "conservative columnist with a liberal flair,"
whose own popular *Let's Get Ahead by Agreeing with All Sides!*
had just been reissued, said, "I agree with all sides." Everyone howled.

There soon followed a chorus from each of the tables, consisting of the word *great*. Everything spoken of was great. People who looked great were great and were doing great things. They also were about to embark on new projects that were in themselves great. At this point I decided to down my second glass of the Jefferson Margaux, which, though it had no taste, nonetheless packed a punch. Just as I was dunking a tournedos into my paella, I caught sight of Chloe at the table for the Perfects. She was giving me the fish eye, as if expecting trouble. Then she turned to Mrs. Bitterman, who was mouthing the word *great*.

After the choir of greatness came a cascade of monologues on topics including the local traffic, the local vegetable and fruit produce, the work one was having done on one's kitchen by locals, and the surprising quality of the local theater. The monologues were followed by laughter, which came in ripples, snorts, hiccups, grunts, gurgles, heehaws, and whinnies. This preceded much chattering and happy screaming, followed by more monologues, followed by whooping and whispering, then tweets and twangs, then nuzzles and side splits, then by more monologues and a moist, ripe belch.

Just when I thought things could not get any more delightful, Mr. Bitterman had a "great idea." Everyone at every table was to stand and tell the others what new great thing he or she was up to.

Vandersnook reported that his likeness was about to appear on a two-cent stamp in Barbados. He said the Barbadian government had originally offered the one-cent, but he had held out and refused to accept anything under two. Everybody clapped and expressed awe at his courage.

Eely Moray, the TV host, was also seated at the Perfect table. A former door-to-door Bible salesman, he wore a red blazer with brass buttons, a boutonniere, and money-green slacks. Eely told the throng that he was giving up television to found his own church based on the teachings of Joseph Campbell. Those who did not comment on how timely his decision was, said it was the bravest thing they had ever heard.

Ben Brio, the garden critic with orchidaceous hair, to whom every weed was a flower and every flower a weed, stood next to deliver the long-awaited news that he had resolved to pull together a collection of his petunia reviews under the title *Brio*. Many guests thought it a daring step. He took the opportunity to thank all the assembled for their too-kind remarks on his first collection, *Luminous*.

Yet more forthcoming books were announced. Truss Inert, the public-relations guru, was hard at work on a groundbreaking study to be called *In Defense of Plagiarists*. This too was regarded as brave. Mack Flecknoe, the fleshy Welsh historian, stood to present his latest, *Harrison: The Only President*

Without a Hagiography. Parkyer Carsir, the gossip publisher, was just getting started on a memoir whose working title was *Will I Ever Get a Seat at the Table?* In response, Mr. Bitterman rose to say, "Well, you'll always have a seat at *our* table, Parkyer." Others chimed in, "You bet!" I recognized Carsir's voice as the one I had heard earlier outside, browbeating Jack.

So it went, round and round. One person said he was planning to take a trip to Belgium in the fall; another was thinking about changing her name to Penny; a third had just become a vegan. All announcements were greeted with equally high enthusiasm. For some reason, the old bat with a cause at my table brought down the house when she said that her effort to protect wheels worldwide had to date raised ten million dollars in donations. And Mr. Jefferson apologized for his wine again, but everyone said it was great anyway.

By now I had guzzled my third glass and was feeling dizzy and queasy to the point of full-blown sickness. The wideboard floors began to morph into the ground level of an abattoir, where bulls and cows and a calf or two were seated at round tables mooing and moaning and kicking up small clouds of dust with their hooves. Smoke plumed from their wide nostrils, which were dilated with fear. Their eyes were bloodshot. I wanted to save the creatures from the farmer in charge of the abattoir, who, scythe in hand, was about to run amok among the animals and slice them to ribbons. But two things stood in my way: I was smashed. And I was the farmer.

Then finally it was my turn to speak. I gulped down my fourth Margaux and decided that I would be more visible and more effective if I stood on the table. In my upward climb I stepped on Pill's wrist and kicked a thick wedge of Key lime pie into the lap of Pasty Williams. Then I told our crowd what I was up to.

"This evening," I said, "this very evening, I am going home to give myself an enema. And it will be great."

Not waiting for the applause, I began to sing, "The Greatest Love of All," gesticulating lavishly in an attempt to get others to join in. Only Mr. Jefferson's new bride obliged. She sang quite well.

To divert attention from me, Mrs. Bitterman hurriedly summoned the cook from the kitchen to receive the plaudits of the guests for preparing such a great dinner. The poor woman blinked furiously as she entered the room, looking like a prisoner who had just been released from solitary confinement into the light. She was tobacco-colored, with glossy brown hair and a very pretty, if terrified, face. To divert attention from *her,* I jumped down from the table, grabbed the male Bitterman, and gave him a long, hard kiss on the mouth. Two kisses, actually: "One for the surf, and one for the turf!"

Chloe rose from her chair like a sergeant reporting for duty. "That's it," she said. "We're going home." As she pushed me toward the door, the Bittermans assured her that everyone understood how I was, and that she mustn't worry about my spoiling the party, and that she, for one, would be welcome in their home at any time, night or day. On our way out, I heard two "Isn't he awful?"s and one "Beyond the pale."

In the driveway, I told Jack the party had been all he'd said it would be, and I gave him a twenty-dollar bill. Chloe said nothing on the ride back to Noman. I said nothing myself, as I was trying to work out a matter that had been troubling me all night.

At last we pulled up at the creek. "You just have to do it, don't you?" she said. "You have to spout off."

"That's it!" I said. "Whales! She was talking about saving the whales!" Then I heaved up the Margaux, the surf and the turf, mostly on Chloe, I'm afraid.

Not long afterward, she announced her departure from our household. Something about a last straw.

At 2:34, the sun no longer equivocates, and has dulled to the color of grade-school glue. The clouds gloom over in the preliminary stages of a rampart, and the day takes on the bleak appeal of a mule, part solemn, part mule. It is a hue I am generally fond of, but now I consider how the inevitable rainstorm may affect the operation of the Da Vinci. Yet it must have rained in the fourth century B.C. too, don't you think? And it's a stolid machine, much more substantial, more structurally austere, than I had ever imagined. When I seek to admire it, it looks away as if to say: You made me, now lay off.

In truth, I had no idea how big and heavy the parts would be, not that the bulk would have deterred me. Sir Ralph's plans, which saw the Da Vinci as a toy involving a Ping-Pong ball, gave specifications in inches. I, possessing a different and grander vision, transposed Sir Ralph's measurements into feet, including the ballistic calculations, which were originally drawn up in meters. The three FedEx packages contained everything from the hinged catch and the winding roller to the massive plates, all ten to twelve times the recommended size.

"Señor Moment!" The bullhorn amplifies every word into a threat. "A question, señor."

"No, José, it isn't Cinco de Mayo yet. But soon. Nine months. You can start preparing the explosives."

"Tell me, Señor. What does that *H* stand for on your horn?"

"It stands for José."

I go to the dock and crawl under the tarp. I am way ahead of schedule. Except for setting and attaching the torsion spring, the project is down to a very few minor touches. I check the ropes. I check the wheels, the mortises for the uprights, the winch crossbar, the mallet, the leg of the catch. I check the pine ball in the tub.

Now to the hill, zip in my stride, ready at last to hook up the horsehair. I feel a surge of satisfaction grading into calm. A shudder of the kind of joy I experienced once in a rare while when I still was writing. What the piano player feels—what Blossom Dearie feels accompanying herself when her voice and fingers meet where they are supposed to—"Is you is or is you ain't my baby?" What the carpenter feels—even the carpenters working on Lapham's—when tongue-and-groove groove. Not pride, exactly. More like control. *Veni, vidi, vici.* Conception, preparation, execution. For one bright-eyed, evanescent moment, control of one's work and of one's art and of one's life.

"I placed a jar in Tennessee, /And round it was upon a hill, / It made the slovenly wilderness . . ." What the *fuck*?

WHAT THE FUCK?

Merely telling you that the Mason jar lies empty on its side, with the horsehair gone, all of it gone, cannot begin to convey my horror and panic at this moment. Neither do I need to ponder the calamity, to attribute it to an accident, or to some natural disaster, or to voodoo, or to divine intervention in the hubris of mortals. Nothing is divine about this theft.

"Hector!"

"What?!" he asks with false innocence, running back to the dock. I go after him.

"What did you do with it?" I loom over him, as if that mattered.

"With what?"

I know he's lying. "The horsehair. Where did you put it?"

He tries to salute. "We have a situation here, General. I'll call the War Room."

"Where is it, dammit?"

"Aren't you ashamed of yourself? A grown man stomping around searching for the hair of a horse? Wouldn't you much prefer the hair of the dog?" I hate it when he chortles.

"Cough it up," I tell him.

"I'm not a cat."

"You didn't eat it! Tell me you didn't eat it."

"I didn't eat it."

I stare at him. "You did. You *did* eat it. Horsehair. Why?"

"Well, for one thing, I'll eat anything, as you surely are aware by now. But if you must know, I'm trying to save you from yourself. What you have in mind will mess up everything for both of us. It's true, I do think we could do a lot better around here, but all in all I happen to like my life the way it is. I'm a conservative, remember."

"How'd you do it?" I ask him, stifling a rage.

"Do what?"

"Get into the jar. How'd you unscrew the top?"

"I prayed it open." He chuckles again.

If a dropkick would bring back the horsehair, he would be dog-paddling in the creek right now. Now that he's mentioned it, though, perhaps I *could* use the hair of this dog in place of the horse's. I'd gladly try, but his hair would be too short. Then again, Sir Ralph's instructions noted that when the ancients had no horsehair available, they used the tendons of any proximate animal. I look Hector over from nose to tail. He bellows, "Oh, what a friend we have in Jesus."

What to do? Months of effort and meticulous planning down the gullet of a cur. *Bang bang bang bang bang.* Is Lapham's house laughing at me?

The bullhorn calls again, "Señor March! We've been talking about you. You seem upset today. Very nervous. More than usual."

"Thank you for your concern, José."

"We theenk you need an activity. Something to keep you busy." Several of the carpenters are looking my way, grinning and nodding in agreement. Their interest in me seems to be growing anthropological. "Maybe you should have a hobby. Maybe you need a woman, señor! But you have to improve your appearance."

"Is that possible?" I wave and head for the house as if I knew what I was doing.

"You definitely need a new shirt, and new shoes. Everytheeing! Even so, we theenk it would take a very patient woman to be with you."

"Did you have someone in mind?" I am about to go inside.

"We were theenking of Señora Polite."

"I'm sure you were."

"But maybe she would be too much woman for a man your age."

Too much for a man of any age, I theenk. And then I think of something else. A vision comes to me in the form of a long, thick, swishy, tail-like braid of hair.

"Is that you, Wrinkles?" she gasps into her end of the phone. "Well! Ah do believe this is the very first time Ah have received a call from your distinguished self."

"It's your lucky day, Chittlins. You have something I want."

"Don't you think it's a bit late for that?" she says. "Late for *you*, Ah mean."

"I want your hair. I want you to cut off that braid of yours and give it to me."

"And why on earth should Ah do that?" she asks. "Ah cannot think for what sick and perverse purpose you could possibly desire mah extra-long, extra-thick, world-class braid of hair."

"I need it. Just leave it at that." I know she won't.

"Are you going to hang yourself? Give me an incentive."

"Never mind why I want it. I'll pay you for it. Plenty. And it will grow back soon. You stand only to profit from this transaction, Kathy."

"Ah worry when you address me by mah Christian name instead of the usual insult, Harry. Ah worry, and yet mah interest is piqued. What do you call plenty?" She is beginning to speak in the short, orgasmic breaths that accompany the sale of a house.

"A thousand dollars," I tell her.

"Ah don't clear mah throat for a thousand dollars." I picture a closed-mouth, cocky smile.

"Five thousand, then." I need to get the deal done.

A sigh of mocking pity seeps through the receiver. "Let me bring you into the twentieth century—or the twenty-first, to be technical about it, my hermit crab."

A chill invades me as I realize that it is she and not I who ought to be addressing the Chautauquans. Like Lapham, Kathy *is* the twentieth century. The two of them ought to be together. They should be wed at once by the Reverend I. Love Everyone in Saint No Offense Church with Hector as their ringbearer. It would be the event of the season. Her wedding gift to him: a morocco-bound volume of *The Collected Aphms*, at long last. His to her: a cash register twenty feet high and twenty wide, on which she could hop from key to key dressed as an adjustable-rate mortgage. On their wedding night, they could dance to Hootie and the Blowfish and watch *Survivor*. He could say: "I want *her* to win." And she: "I want *him*."

She inhales and continues. "For your edification, Harry March, five thousand dollars these days will not suffice as a deposit to take a house off the market for a single night. On an average sale—an *average* sale, mind you—one that takes me as long as ten minutes to consummate—mah commission comes to four hundred thousand dollars. And do you know that in order to hold that cashier's check for four hundred thousand dollars in my delicate-as-china hand, Ah do not need to lose a single hair on mah oh-so-desirable head?"

I ought to get out more. If I knew more people, or even knew *of* more people, I would never have had to approach Ms. Southern Discomfort in the first place. Maybe I should have gone into real estate myself; imagined estate has proved to be far less practical.

The urge arrives to gather up everything Southern and dump it on her from an extreme altitude—levees, gumbo, étouffée, catalpa trees, sweating Mississippi courtrooms with redneck juries composed of men named Wayne and slowly revolving ceiling fans, cicadas, hoop skirts, mud, buckshot, whips, bayous, verandas, juleps (mint and original), hooch, "Swanee," Big Daddy's white suit, Big Daddy, and Big Daddy's house—just lift it all by crane, open the claws, let it drop, and bury her forever, except for that braid.

The hour grows late. I'm sunk if she doesn't come through. It could take me weeks to find and prepare more horsehair, and by then Lapham's house will be open for business. The Quiogue stables can't help me now; their horses have just had haircuts. I suppose I could look on eBay, but there's no time for delivery even by FedEx, which anyway, I am certain, has put me on its blacklist.

What must be done must be done tonight, before tomorrow morning's lecture to the Chautauquans. How else can I show them the way? And if I don't show them, how will they show others? My subversion is a small gesture, to be sure, but it will make a statement, an impression. Worlds of thought and action have been moved by less, have been revolutionized by more obscure acts than mine. Believe me. Check your history. Besides, I refuse to give up now, after my bounty of headaches, backaches, earaches, toothaches (from holding the flashlight), scraped knees, bloody hands and feet, frayed nerves, heartburn, sleepless nights, and *bang-bang* days. It's been too much fun.

"All right. How much *do* you want?"

"Why, Ah want *you*, honey." I picture her spreading open her arms like Aimee Semple McPherson. "Ah want your house, your island, the works. And Ah'll pay top dollar."

"Because you can turn it around and get back twice what you give me," I feebly suggest.

"Three times. Maybe four. You sell me your little Island of Dr. Moreau, and Ah'll pay you enough to enable you to live out your shriveled, mean-spirited days in the comfort of the finest assisted-living facility on the East End, with plenty of dollars to spare in case you want to take a day trip to the Ausable Chasms or catch a bus to see a revival of *Cats*. And for all that, Ah shall gladly cut off my luxurious braid of hair and hand it over to you mahself."

"Never!" I shout into the phone.

"Harry March!" she shouts back, making my name sound like two imperatives. "You're hurtin' me! Never say never." Another intake of breath. There's a pause. Then: "Ah must say, Ah get all hot just thinkin' what you might be planning on doing with mah hair."

"You'd be surprised," I tell her. "What about fifty thousand? It's all I have." I may be lying to her; I don't really know. Hector says we're rich, but he can only count to seven. I haven't checked the Money Room in quite a while. In any case, her reply makes the effort unnecessary.

"This conversation is concluded. Sell me your island, and mah hair is yours. Your island. Your house." She means my life. "That's mah price, sweet pea." She hangs up, and my heart sinks with the click.

I look down at my little white anarchist, cold as I can look.

"Thanks a lot, Hector." He seems enthused by what he has overheard.

"*De nada*," he says. "Well, so much for the Da Vinci." He tries unsuccessfully to rub his front paws together. "Now you can drop the lecture too. Isn't that good? You can't do one without the other."

"That's right, rub it in."

"But I've provided you with the perfect out. You can tell them your dog ate your homework."

"You know," I tell him as I head for my rowboat, "for a self-proclaimed born-again Christian, you practice very little charity."

He wags his euphoric tail. "Now why don't you just forget all this nonsense—forget Kathy's braid, forget your crazy plot—and calm down and concentrate on little Hector, devote your remaining days to ensuring little Hector's happiness and welfare? I'll take you to church with me, and you'll see the light and learn to love Jesus and America, and then you can write a best-seller about a dog who talks to God. And it'll make us lots of money, so we can buy Lapham's house and live in the lap of luxury. I love laps."

"You're very annoying, you know."

"We're *both* very annoying. That's why we're friends."

"Are we friends?"

He gives me the Quizzical head tilt. "Of course we're friends."

Eleven

Get your leash."

"I hate that," he says.

"You hate your leash?"

"I hate the fact that I automatically obey certain things you say. That you programmed me when I was too young to resist."

"Those were the days." I have no time for this. "Get your leash. We're going to town." I climb in the boat.

" 'Get your leash,' " he grumbles. " 'Get your leash.' 'Lie down.' 'Heel!' Imagine ordering someone to heel! 'Beg!' Imagine ordering someone to beg!" One day I taught him about Pavlov, and he hit the ceiling.

"Are you coming or not?" I know he is; he lunges at any opportunity to get off the island. He crouches where the platforms meet on the dock, then springs into the rowboat, seeming briefly like an ordinary dog. "Good boy!" I tell him, though I know I always have to pay, one way or another, for needling Hector.

The phone rings as I am about to untie the ropes from the cleats on the pilings. Maybe Kathy's calling back. Leaving Hector in the boat, I move as quickly as I can up the beach, up the lawn, and into the house. I get to the phone on the seventh ring.

"Well? Have you changed your mind?" I ask.

A strangely arresting silence follows. "Not bloody likely," says the voice at the other end of the line.

"Chloe?" I find myself standing straighter.

"Harry, the children called me about your e-mail. They're very worried, and so am I."

"Oh, no no no no, Chlo. Everything is great."

"Joel is worried too."

"I've never met Joel," I say, as if that comes to her as news. "But if the event I'm planning requires a professional touch, I'll be sure to let him know."

"He's worried because *I'm* worried," she says, putting me in my place. "Harry, please try to focus. You're sounding crazier and crazier. I don't know what you're planning, and I know you won't tell me, but promise me you won't do something stupid or dangerous."

I remain quiet.

"Harry?"

"Chloe, I'm very grateful for the call. Give my thanks to Joel too. And I apologize for the wisecrack. But I was just about to go off island. May I call you back tomorrow? We'll have a nice long chat."

"That was both gracious and coherent, Harry. Now you've *really* got me scared. I hardly need to remind you that you're the last one to determine that you're okay."

I'd put up an argument if she were wrong.

"Harry, I love you. The children love you. Whatever it is you're doing, please remember that there are people who care about you." Her voice cracks. "I'll leave it at that."

"Got to go, Chlo," I tell her, my voice also cracking. I'll leave that at that, too.

As I'm about to climb back into the boat, Hector looks up. "I heard you say Chloe. Did she mention me?"

"Yes. She asked if you were still alive."

"Praise the Lord!" he says. "She was thinking about little Hector!"

I guide us outside the *L* of the dock, brace my feet against the ribs of the boat and ply the oars with deep and even strokes. Four minutes from shore to shore across the Styx. Dave, Jack, and the Mexicans declare their surprise at the sight of us, since I only ever leave Noman to buy provisions, twice a month. The Mexicans greet Hector as they might Zapata. He in turn does his usual Mexican hat dance of excitement. Their fondness for him is ethnic-based; I once told them I'd named him after all of them.

Even when I do go off island, I rarely travel far. Usually I shop either at the little country market in Quogue, to which I can easily walk once I get across the creek, or at the supermarket in Westhampton Beach, to which I can hitch. Ravioli and Devil Dogs, I have discovered, are obtainable everywhere. Today, however, I need Southampton, second to Riverhead as largest town in the area. Like most Hamptons towns, it has been manufactured for people at play, and is the likeliest place, I have reckoned, to find a solution to my problem.

Tied up at Lapham's dock, which is sufficiently large to accommodate six Love Boat cruise ships complete with viruses and rapists, is a sleek forty-foot job of blue fiberglass and radiant teak and cherry. I put in next to it, jetsam beside the *Isle de France*.

"You know what that is?" Dave asks. Of course I do not. "It's a Hinckley Picnic Boat, the best powerboat in the world. Draft is six inches. Has both gas and jet engines. Costs four hundred and fifty thousand bucks."

"Put me down for two," I tell him.

Up close, Lapham's construction site appears more menacing than it does from Noman. It is worse than a mythical animal. It is real, and has grown into a village; no, a city; no, a nation-state erupting from the soil to assert its dominance and flex its muscle. The eyeless cavities of the windows await glass. The vast, mouthy entranceway is ready to receive the double portals. The steps to the Parthenon are in place, as are the chimneys, all twelve of them. It goes on forever, the flagstone pathways leading to outbuildings and more outbuildings, including an indoor basketball court (heated, says Dave) and a garage for fifty cars (also heated). A putting green. A tower. A moat. A chapel. The bomb shelter. Where are the slave quarters? Where is the prison? And off to the side of the pool house, the Tilles Blowhard, dark and lethal, points its black hole at me like one of the guns of Navarone. Krento was right: the house is nearly done.

"Yet another room?" I ask. On the left wing of the monstrosity, Dave's men are hammering away at a structure in the shape of a top-heavy X, with circles at the shorter tips. It looks like a distorted pair of scissors.

"Uh-huh," says Dave. "At the last minute he decided he wanted a special room to exhibit his collection of antique asparagus tongs, if you can believe it."

"I can."

"Leave Hector with us," says one of the carpenters.

"Only if you promise to mistreat him." Hector and I skirt Lapham's property and head for the road, where we'll catch the bus to Southampton.

"Be careful, Harry," Dave calls after us. "You're going out into the world."

"Das right," says José. "Ees not like your island. Ees a jungle out there. Anything can happen."

"True. I may run into some Mexicans." They talk to me as if I were a child. I may not be as smooth as some, but I can certainly handle myself in Southampton, for God's sake.

We leave the Lapham empire and walk along Quogue Street, or as it was known in my youth, Main Street, which, in the eighteenth century, served as a wide, flat drag for sheep and cows when Quogue was a patchwork of farms. Past former boardinghouses for seaside seekers in the 1920s and 1930s since gutted and remolded into bulbous single dwellings. Past more grand houses under repair, or in the ecstasies of expansion, or wholly new constructions wrapped in white Dupont Tyvek building paper, used to repel moisture and dampness, and me. Tyvek. The word covers the Hamptons. The signature of King Tyvek the Mummifier, the Mummy himself. Bandages shredded and askew, he bursts from his sarcophagus and mauls the wooded lots. The deer flee, crazed.

The constructions rise on brown, yet-to-be-landscaped grounds among the building permits, contractor signs ("You Dream It, We Build It"), and a thinned-out forest of green Porta Pottis. One fine day, a million sprinklers will erupt in unison and announce the houses' grand openings. Like Lapham's, these junior mansions all have massive (if fewer) fieldstone chimneys, Potemkin porches on which no one ever will rock, and rococo balconies over their front doors. Interspersed among the older houses, they stand looking vaguely related to one another, like the overweight children of a demented family.

Past the khaki-shingled Church of the Atonement (Episcopal, 1884), with its stained glass saints and angels, where my mother prayed, mainly for my father, who would not have set foot in that or any other "house of superstition" if his life had depended on it. Past the Inn at Quogue, which changes management every year or so in search of the perfect Bloody Mary.

Past Jessup Avenue, Quogue's one-block "business section." When so much is new or renewed in one's hometown, one feels the imprint of places no longer there—more pentimento than palimpsest. That's where the schoolhouse used to be. That's where Tommy Trudeau, my boyhood buddy, lived, before his family moved back to Indiana. And so on. Now one in three buildings houses a real estate broker. I pull

Hector quickly past Polite for the Elite so that we can avoid
the haranguing voice of Dixie.

Past the Quogue Free Library, before whose entrance lies
the great rusted iron anchor from the schooner *Nahum
Chapin* that went down off Quogue Beach in 1897, all hands
lost. Mrs. Damato the librarian sees Hector and me walking
by as she is about to enter the building. It was she who gave
me my first library card, led me to Swift, scolded me for doing cannonballs from the Post Bridge, and stood beside my
parents at the train station when I went off to college. She
served the same purposes for Charles, Emma, and James. I
nod to her respectfully. She smiles sardonically.

"You used to be such a sweet little boy, Harry. What happened?"

"The war," I tell her, and move on.

"Tell me again," Hector says impatiently as we arrive at the
highway and wait for the bus in the dense afternoon heat. "We
do not own a car because . . . ?"

"Because we don't need one," I explain for the hundredth
time.

"Oh yes! The bus is so much more convenient. Why can't
we take the bus with the hair dryers?"

He's referring to a special luxury jitney that runs between
New York City and the Hamptons, a mobile beauty parlor
where women get peeled, waxed, manicured, pedicured,

massaged, and blown dry for the evening parties they are riding toward.

"Because it doesn't use this route. And it's idiotic," I tell him.

"To you, everything comfortable is idiotic." He rubs the side of his head with his paw. "When we're in town, can I go to Puppy Pompadour?"

"No. You look fine."

"Can I ever go to Puppy Pompadour?"

"No."

The county bus system on the East End may be a pathetic enterprise, as he suggests, but it affords useful transportation for those of us whose Bentleys are in the shop. A wounded fleet of small and scarred buses—steel-blue, pea-green, and dirty-white in color—sputters up and down the northern and southern jaws of the alligator all day long, like pacing penitents. On the southern jaw they rattle along the Old Montauk Highway, so called to distinguish it from Route 27, Sunrise Highway, which runs roughly parallel a few miles to the north. As late as the 1950s, the Old Montauk Highway was the main road out to the Hamptons; the Long Island Expressway, known as the LIE, did not extend this far east until 1972. The drive from the city to Southampton took between four and five hours, and getting to East Hampton, which seemed as distant as Portugal, required much of the day.

That was when the Hamptons still served as the salty spa of

the old-money rich (including Lapham's ancestors, no doubt), whose convoys of black-and-maroon Packard limousines and woody station wagons crept out along the Montauk Highway in late May, not to return to the brass-plated doorways of the Park and Fifth Avenue apartment houses and maisonettes till after Labor Day. Today Hector and I ride an old bus on an old road known as Old.

The bus shimmies to a muffled ticking, steady as a metronome. *Tick tick tick*. Our only fellow passengers are a pair of day laborers, too exhausted to speak, in paint-splattered jeans. One slaps at a fly that has landed on his knee. They slump and stare. We roll past tiny houses with cobwebs in the corners of their windows, where retired insurance agents live with their complete sets of the *Book of Knowledge* and bathrobes pilfered from a Marriott. At night their TVs flicker blue.

On the shoulders of the road are women, mostly, walking slowly and alone or burdened with plastic grocery bags and children. In Africa or in the Caribbean, they would be carrying their goods on their heads. They are pin-spotted by the midafternoon sun, whose light grows weaker as the clouds thicken. They move in a platinum haze. Back they go to their rooms with plywood walls above the tanning salons and stores that sell painted chambered nautiluses, or to their trailer parks, discreetly screened behind a bulwark of foliage.

This is the *other* life of the Hamptons, the life that is neither the leisured life nor the life that supports it. This is the single-mother life, the life on the dole, of Social Security checks and retirement checks, and rented bedroom sets with pineapples carved in their headboards, and bargain coupons clipped from newspapers for Goya beans and Fresca. It hangs its head and goes about its business like a secret government agency, as hidden as, yet less essential to the lives of other Hamptonites than, propeller blades on boats or the linings of private jets.

Hector sits and takes it in. The bus bumps east from Quogue, and in and out of East Quogue, a town that has gussied itself up over the past few years with turn-of-the-century street lamps, craft shops, frequent street fairs, a shop that sells expensive handmade dollhouses, and a village green dotted with old-fashioned benches with wrought iron arms and featuring a spiffy playground for toddlers. For life's other extreme, a development for "lively adults" (which I assume means that no wheelchairs or walkers are permitted) crowds the cleared acres north of the highway. Brand-new, it nonetheless gives off the aura of an abandoned Massachusetts factory that once produced hats or shoes on an assembly line alongside a polluted river.

Motels named Something Cottages and Something Court, a miniature golf, a Sunoco station, a Citgo, King Kullen and his Dairy Queen, Beach Limos, Beach Chiropractic, Sandy Man (cleans private beaches), a day spa, a spa store (offering "leak detection and liner replacement"), a car wash, a place that sells Bilko doors, and an Al-Anon center. Brief flashes of goldenrod, beach plum, and pepperbush. We enter Hampton Bays, which changed its name from Good Ground in 1922 to Hamptonize itself. Fortunately for the citizens, the name-change did not do the trick. Today the town encompasses a new shopping mall and old Italians who still live to fish. At night in the summer, teenage boys with sideburns shaved above their ears loiter around the entrance to the movie theater, while girls with matted mascara and cotton-candy hair lean against the wall of the pizzeria, waiting for the scuba instructor of their dreams. The sidewalk wobbles with weekend celebrants from share houses, and the whole town stinks of beer. But on the quiet little streets south of the highway are real people doing real things and leading real lives with real problems. And at the tail ends of those streets that drop off into Shinnecock Bay, Hampton Bays becomes an old gentleman with impeccable manners dressed in a black suit, ready for Mass.

No homeless people to be seen today, strangely enough. They exist in Hampton Bays, but are almost nonexistent in the posher villages. Several summers ago a homeless man was spotted wandering on the grounds of the Meadow Club in

Southampton. The members did not know what to do with him, so they threw him a party.

"Which Hampton is your favorite?" asks Hector, not faintly interested in my response. He does this sort of thing often—plays the innocent acolyte in pursuit of instruction when he seeks to distract me from a mission.

"None of them," I tell him. "That's why we live in Quogue."

"Isn't Quogue a Hampton?"

"By general location, yes. But Quogue is too dull to qualify as a real Hampton."

In a way, it is snobbish and preposterous to favor one village over another; all have the same money, put to the same uses, though there are small distinguishing characteristics. Remsenberg has the enchantment of a hotel corridor; Westhampton, of a demimondaine who has come into money; and East Hampton, of one's exotic first lover: wears short skirts, speaks French, and dumb as a post.

Quogue remains the best of the lot for me, because it still honors privacy. To the citizens of Quogue, "How are you?" is intrusive. They greet one another with "Morning" because they do not wish to commit themselves to the prefatory "Good." Of course, Lapham's rollicking presence will change all that.

"You're telling me, it's dull," he says. "That's why we're there, isn't it? Because nothing ever happens."

"I wouldn't say that."

"Why do you suppose Mr. Lapham is settling in Quogue?" He knows I resent the "Mr." "And please don't tell me he's there to destroy the universe."

"I don't know. Quogue is WASPier, I suppose."

"What does that mean, 'waspy'?"

"That's what we are: WASPs."

"I'm a wasp?"

"Don't worry about it."

"I'm a wasp like Mr. Lapham?" He goes quiet. His silences are more unnerving than his talk. "What goes on in East Hampton?" he asks.

"Noise, gossip, and construction."

"What goes on in Bridgehampton?"

"Noise, gossip, and construction."

"And Westhampton?"

"Westhampton has noise and construction."

"Why no gossip?"

"Periodontists don't gossip. Say, isn't it time for one of your thirty daily naps?"

"Actually, I'm feeling quite awake today," he says, shaking himself off as if he were wet. "Quite peppy! Full of life! It must be something I ate." I am very glad he cannot smirk. "Why isn't there a Northampton?" he asks.

"Because it's against the law to locate a Hampton north of

the highway." I make a show of turning away from him. We tick tick tick past shrink-wrapped powerboats stacked like dead great whites at the edge of the road. They create their own fluorescence. I feel a pang of discouragement.

The final leg of the twenty-minute trip covers a stretch of road that runs over the Shinnecock Canal, created when the hurricane of 1938 cut a chunk out of the base of the southern jaw, and then another stretch where the Old Montauk Highway becomes Hill Street, a sudden boulevard with trees that bloom like broccoli and many substantial homes on both sides built in the idiom of the region. Hill Street constitutes the gateway to Southampton as well as the northerly border of what is probably the ritziest estate section on Long Island and second only to Newport as the birthplace of American hoity-toity. Here one may drive through alleys of linden trees, Bradford pears, and maples, all the same sculpted height, then turn left or right and crawl another quarter of a mile down white-pebble driveways to arrive at imitation Monticellos that were the precursors of Lapham's current imitation. Only eyes clouded by sentiment see these pillared show-offs as being less outlandish than Lapham's. Architecturally more pleasing, they nonetheless arise from the same wolfish appetite.

In this estate section, as in similar select spas throughout the country, originated the summer "cottages"—a name that once accurately described modest bungalows attached to grand resort hotels in the 1870s and 1880s. These bona fide cottages became so popular that when the exceedingly rich decided to build their own vast homes in the quasi-pastoral idylls, they retained the generic designation. The new cottages were given names that contradicted their cottageness— *Bellefontaine, Sans Souci,* and *Beaulieu*—which eventually evolved into awkward little joke names such as *Casa Ra Sera* and *Me and My Chateau,* and further down the ladder, to *Villa Ever Payphor Dis.* (In Gresham's Law of House Names, stupidest drives out stupider.) I heard that Lapham, as a gesture of familial gratitude, intended to name his cottage either *Holy Moses* or *Tongs a Lot.*

"Tell me about the Hamptons again. Tell me about Southampton. We haven't spoken of Southampton."

"Perfumed candles and fudge," I tell him.

"That's all you have to say about Southampton?"

I nod.

Southampton has the seductive apathy of a debutante, but none of the appealing cruelty. I have always pictured the world ending there: the doors of the shops squawk on their hinges. The eaves of the roofs sag with debris. The druggist's shelves are covered with thick dust caught in a prismatic light, and the white and pink summer dresses in the dress shops sway on their racks. Nothing remains of the bank but its vault, the door open, the cash in a flutter. Nothing remains of the schoolyard but the jungle gym and the chain-link fence that has been yanked from its stanchions. The distant ocean hisses like steam in a pipe, and a fragment of a red merino sweater clings to a bush.

"I like Southampton," he says.

"Good. We're almost there." Sensing that I am about to solve the horsehair problem, he hopes we'll miss our stop.

"What do Hamptonites do in the daytime?" he asks.

"They speak of their careers."

"Why do they do that?"

"It makes them happy. Sometimes they advance their careers by speaking to other Hamptonites. That's why they live here."

"That's nice."

"No, it isn't."

"But isn't a career important?"

"Not when it interferes with a life."

"What else do Hamptonites do in the daytime?" He appears puppylike when it suits him.

"They make themselves beautiful."

"And what else?"

"They prepare to go to parties, or to throw parties."

"And what else?"

"They dream up great works."

"What comes of them?"

"Nothing."

"And what else?"

"They hope that other Hamptonites are thinking of them. And that everyone is thinking well of them."

"And are they?"

"No and no."

I don't want to go into it with him, but as the Bittermans' dinner party demonstrated, the thinking can get unusual in places like this. In any discriminating society, my behavior on that evening ought to have led to my permanent expunction from any and all future invitation lists. Instead, it ensured my popularity, and since that time I doubt there has been a single Hamptons event—including the highly selective DeMott Club's "Tribute to the Fox-trot" and Mrs. Epstein's "Night of New York Geniuses"—to which I have not been asked. (The Bittermans themselves have come close to begging.) Had my case of typhlitis improved, of course, I would gladly have attended them all.

"Tell me about other places."

"That's enough." I let the driver know that we're about to get off.

"Tell me about Massapequa." He knows the name of the midalligator town only because he was born there and that was where I acquired him. I have always wondered if his breeder knew more than he let on; he charged me half price.

"Tell me about Shelter Island."

"Look." My exasperation clearly gratifies him. "They're all the same. The Hamptons are all the same. And that includes the towns that you have not yet mentioned but undoubtedly intend to, Water Mill, Sagaponack, Wainscott, North Haven, North Sea Harbor, Noyack, and Amagansett.

"Basically, they are all the same. The same shops, the same roads, the same trees, the same geraniums in the same pots, the same Sub-Zeros and Wolfs, the same inlaid tile, the same recessed lighting, the same photographs of families at play in the same pickled wood frames, the same people wearing the same outfits, the same prattle, the same shellacked faces, the same howler monkeys brachiating from event to event, the same opinions on the same issues, the same hummus with the same chips, the same unconscious despair crouching behind the privet hedges."

"Oh, no!" he says. "Not another lecture. Can't you save it for the Chautauquans?"

"You brought up the subject, so you get the subject."

"I was only trying to pass the time on a summer's day," he lies.

"That's right. The Hamptons are all the same, and all of

America is the same, and all the world wants to be like all of America so that it too can be the same." He covers his ears with his front paws. But I persist: "The same definition of happiness, the same personal lusts, the same idea of what passes for achievement, the same disregard for value and virtue and honor, the same hollowness at the core.

"And do you know who embodies, who symbolizes, who generates and perpetuates this universal vacuity?"

"I do, but you're going to tell me anyway, aren't you?"

"Correct. It's Lapham!"

"No!"

"Yes!"

"Such a lovely day!" He sticks his little head out the bus window and contemplates the heavens. The tuberous clouds have closed ranks, and the sky is shut as tight as the hatch on an army tank.

Twelve

It is uniquely irritating for me to walk with Hector in public places because inevitably there will be people who recognize him and call out his name in affectionate and admiring tones. This is due to the lamentable fact that shortly after I acquired him, I made the error of writing an essay about him for *The New Yorker*, which drew him considerable and undeserved attention. Because the essay appeared in *The New Yorker*, people who wished to seem sophisticated felt they had been extended an intellectual invitation to participate in it. And because I portrayed Hector as being exceptionally intelligent and adorable (this was before his religious conversion) and cast myself as his amused factotum, total strangers have ever since felt free to address him on sight and to ignore me. Only the latter treatment has been welcome.

So it is, as we proceed down Main Street, that several people shout out "Hector!" (His name seems to require a shout.)

And "Hector, old buddy!" And "Hector, my man!" To all this he responds with the fluffy narcissism of an entrant in a dog show, which consigns me to the vassalage of one of those mute and buoyant trainers in sneakers trotting by his side.

He takes a leak on everything vertical that is not human, including but not limited to trees, telephone poles, wooden posts, hydrants, and bus stops. "I'm going to own this town," he says.

"Just make sure all your expulsions come from that orifice." I forgot to bring baggies. "I'm going in here."

He sniffs up. "Reigning Cats & Dogs? Great!" He likes pet stores because he views them as opportunities to proselytize the other animals.

"*I'm* going. You're staying out here in the street."

"But why?" he asks, cocking his head in the How-Cute-Am-I? tilt.

"Hector! You the man!" An aging male zeppelin in a green tank top floats by, too cool for words.

"See?" says Hector. "I'm the man."

"You are nothing like a man, Mr. Tail. That's why you are not coming into the pet store. See that sign?" He can see it, but he can't read it. "It says: 'No food or drinks, no bare feet, no evangelicals.'" He sits down on the sidewalk outside Reigning Cats and Dogs, turns his head away from me, and welcomes additional shouts of fealty from passersby.

"Do you carry horsehair, or something close to it?" I ask the Orville Redenbacher behind the counter.

" 'Close to it,' you mean like the horse?" A kindred spirit. "What are you looking to do?"

In broad terms, I tell him about the torsion spring.

"We have plenty of dog and cat hair. But that's not what you need." He frowns like a drowned cigar. "Know where you can find horsehair?" I do not. "In the walls!" He swings an arm to indicate the walls of his shop.

"What do you mean?" It is chastening for me to meet a *genuinely* crazy person. I ask him to clarify his statement.

"In the nineteenth century," he explains, "they used real plaster on walls and ceilings."

"And?"

"And to keep the plaster intact and make sure it would adhere to the frame, they stuck in horsehair as it hardened."

"You're kidding. So any house more than a hundred years old will still have horsehair in its walls right now?" I ask him.

"That's right. Take a sledgehammer to any nineteenth-century house—any *original* nineteenth-century house, not one that's been renovated—and you'll find all the horsehair you could ever need."

So taken am I with this information that upon returning to the sidewalk, I make the mistake of relating it to Hector. He overreacts. "Terrific!" he says. "By all means, let's knock down the walls of the house so you'll have everything you need to commit a crime." I try to pull him along by his leash, but he digs in with his hind feet. "The wages of sin," he says. " 'Maketh a plan for revenge and bringeth thine own house down upon thine head.' "

"Or upon thine," I cheerfully point out.

We walk past desultory tourists deep in private prayer that they will catch a glimpse of Renée Zellweger. A Piper Cub drones overhead, trailing a long red-and-black pennant advertising *Live for Today*, which I interpret as a personal communication until I see that it's an ad for the morning television show. Gulls turned buzzards screak on the rims of the village trash cans, flap their aggressive wings, and do not scare. People pause before the windows of a shop displaying paintings of lighthouses and in front of the cheese shop. A man has sundered himself from his strolling party to gaze at a display of Stilton. Shuffle and stop, stop and shuffle. It all feels like a muffled dance of the dead, intensified, not relieved by, an occasional outcry of greeting. I hear lifers calling to one another from the caged windows of their cell doors. But that's just me.

Play It Again, the town toy store, is down the street from Reigning Cats & Dogs. Beyond it lie Watch It, the jewelry shop; Love All, the tennis shop; Picture This, the framing shop; Flower Power; and Hair Today. All the stores have stage names except Bookhampton, whose name I've always admired because it seems to suggest a Hampton composed entirely of books. Nuts 'n' Bolts, the hardware store, Song 'n' Dance, the music store. Not long ago, I proposed to a cop on the beat that the police and fire departments be yoked together under the name Shoots 'n' Ladders, but he seemed uninterested.

Writer's Crock, briefly a chichi restaurant, now has whitewash slathered on its windows and a boarded-up door. Last spring, in an effort to create what she called a Gustatory Athenaeum for the Written Word, a garrulous groupie aptly named Lipman inaugurated it as an establishment whose only patrons were to be writers, along with a smattering of media types who would make note of the writers present. As a special touch, she drew the menu from recipes detailed in well-known books, among them Faulkner's braised cuttlefish, Dreiser's kumquat stew, and a dish of boiled shoes described in *The Gulag Archipelago*. The restaurant closed after six weeks, not because the writers had grown tired of their own company or the media people of reporting on them, but because a dozen customers were hospitalized with food poisoning.

The toy store allows dogs, so I let Hector tag along. But the answer comes up negative here as well.

"No. No horsehair. We do have a very nice hobbyhorse, but it's hairless." The woman clerk, who frightens me on sight, bears a terrible resemblance to a photographer who once approached me at a reading. She had Medusa's exploding hair and an expression blending anger with desire. She wanted to take my picture for future book jackets and kept flying at me as though I were a liquidation sale. If I'd had four other guys with me at the time, I would have slugged her.

When I inform the clerk that the hobbyhorse will not do, she takes the news as a personal rebuke and sulks into a copy of *Glamour*.

But on the counter I do see something of interest: a doll about a foot tall, with big brown eyes, overdressed in a yellow satin gown, a yellow beaded necklace, and a conical hat from the middle of which protrudes a pink plastic ruby.

"It comes with a wand," says the clerk, revived by my attention to the doll. "Go ahead. Touch the wand to the ruby." Music plays, and the doll starts to speak. "Isn't she adorable?" the woman says. "She's called Fairy Tale Dora. Dora—you know, Dora the Explorer?" I tell her I do not. "Oh! Dora is very popular. Children love her videos. She speaks English and Spanish."

"Does she do construction work?" And before she can give me a straight answer, I see Dora's hair growing out of her cone crown. The hair gleams in a braid like Kathy Polite's. In fact, Dora looks a good deal like Kathy but seems kinder and better educated. There must be ten inches of hair sprouting from her head. "It feels quite real," I comment to the clerk, whose eyes begin to narrow. I rub the hair between my index finger and my thumb to test its strength. I twist it into a torsion spring. I rub it some more. I sing, "Oh, you beautiful doll, you great big beautiful doll," holding my bandaged ear like a band singer of the 1920s. The smile has vanished from the clerk's countenance.

"You seem to like the doll," she says, her lips tightening. "This would be something for your granddaughter?"

"No."

"A niece? The child of a friend?"

"No, I'd like it for myself," I tell her. "I'll take four." That should do it. I keep stroking the hair. The woman backs away. "How much?" I ask.

She glances around the store as if searching for backup. "You know," she says finally, "I just remembered: we're all out of Fairy Tale Doras." I hold up the doll in both hands as evidence of her error. "And we are forbidden to sell the floor sample." More looking around the room. "I, uh, I could order four dolls for you."

"But I need them today," I insist, hoping that my enthusiasm may persuade her to bend store policy. It seems to have the opposite effect. Hector tugs on his leash and whispers, "Let's get out of here."

"Well," says the clerk, her eyes now flicking from side to

side like pinballs. She is appearing more Medusa-like by the second; the locks of her hair are aflame. "Perhaps I could check the inventory downstairs."

"Never mind," I tell her. With petulant resignation, I reposition Fairy Tale Dora on the shelf. It is 3:51. I'm getting nowhere.

"You really are crazy," says Hector when we're out on the street again. "You'll get us tossed in jail." He may be right. When we've gone twenty yards or so, I turn back toward the toy store, at whose front door I see Medusa speaking with a policewoman pointing in my direction. I take the high road and move on, as if I could not guess what they're discussing.

"Let's look in One More Time," says Hector. He is eager to get off the street. One More Time is an elegant secondhand shop that sells stuff once owned by the old-rich families of the area. Over the years it has become an accidental and transitional repository of Southampton folklore. When one of the great cottages is demolished to make room for a newer and larger monstrosity such as Lapham's, the contents are often sold to One More Time, which in turn sells them to newcomers. Thus does the High Life stay aloft in remnants, as photographs of the Whiffenpoofs of 1928 or of the St. Paul's lacrosse team (all wearing beanies), or cast-iron doorstops in the shape of Scotties or rabbits, or stacks of pinkish cake plates, or tiny tarnished silver spoons are passed down to those who wish to acquire the old world here, much as they do by way of the calculated fantasies of Ralph Lauren.

Hector, I am certain, regards whatever time we might spend in this shop as another delaying tactic. But I know that unusual things may be found here, so I ask the horsehair question as we enter.

"You will not believe this," says the proprietor, a sharp and witty woman who always appears to be looking me over as a potential future piece of merchandise. "We were given a hatbox full of horsehair only last week."

"A hatbox full of horsehair!" I repeat. We seem equally excited, though I soon discover it is not for the same reason.

"A hatbox full of horsehair," she says again. "Mrs. Livingston, of Gin Lane? Do you know her?" It comes to her that she is talking to me. "Oh. I guess not. Anyway, Mrs. Livingston discovered the hatbox in her attic. It belonged to her husband's grandmother, also Mrs. Livingston." I attempt to wave away the mesmerizing biography of the Livingstons. "Well, sir. She discovered a hatbox full of horsehair."

"Please do not say it again," says Hector.

"Yes! It seems that the older Mrs. Livingston wanted to preserve the hair of her favorite jumper, a gelding named Mr. Huey, after Mr. Huey went lame and had to be shot."

"A hatbox full of horsehair!" I repeat deliberately. "Well, my dear. You have a sale." For a moment I allow myself to think my tide may be turning, and I offer a silent thanks to the gelded Mr. Huey and the sentimental Mrs. Livingston.

"But that is the part you won't believe," says the woman, and in so doing indicates that my brief taper of happiness is about to be snuffed out. "I sold the hatbox this very morning!"

"No!" I cry.

"Yes!" she cries back. She assumes I am reacting to the co-incidence rather than to a catastrophe. "Do you know a couple named Lapham?" she asks. My cheekbones freeze over, my left eyelid twitches, and all my cells go dry. "Well, it seems that Mrs. Lapham makes her own throw pillows, and when I told her about the horsehair, she grabbed it up. It makes a perfect stuffing."

"Doesn't it," says Hector.

"It's very sweet, really. She's is making a pillow as a sur-prise for Mr. Lapham and is planning to present him with it on the occasion of the completion of their new house. I hear it's magnificent. It's quite near your island, actually."

"Is that so?" Hector snickers.

"And the whole thing was pure luck: she'd come in for a pair of Victorian asparagus tongs, but then she saw the horsehair. Of course, it was ideal. Such a nice story," she goes on. "The Laphams had a dog who died last year. Why, it was just like your little Hector! A Westie!" Up shoot those ears. "So Mrs. Lapham, knowing how Mr. Lapham adored their dog, is embroidering a picture of it on the cover of the pillow. You never saw anyone happier than she was when she took hold of that hatbox full of horsehair. Providence, she said. She called it Providence."

"Amen, sister," says Hector. I drag him out of the store.

"We're going home," I tell him.

He sees a gregarious Jack Russell down the street and begins barking furiously at him.

"May I ask why you do that?"

"Do what?"

"Bark at the sight of another dog."

"Because other dogs bark at *me.*"

"Yes, but *why*?"

"I don't know," he says, eyeing me as if I had asked him the stupidest question in history.

"You don't see me flying off the handle when I spot another human being."

"Actually, I do." I drop the subject. "You're giving up?" he asks hopefully.

"Not a chance." Armed with the information provided by the pet store proprietor, I am eager to get back to Noman.

Hector senses this. I glance down. "No! Please!" Without warning, he has assumed a take-a-dump squat at the base of a venerable sweet gum.

"How could I resist?" he says, completing his deposit. "Did you get a whiff of this tree?"

The Jack Russell, who has now parked himself in front of the toy store, lets fly again. Hector balances upright against the taut leash, then takes off after him, pulling free from my grip. I pursue him to the Jack Russell, reaching him just as Medusa emerges from the shop and starts yelling at me, her finger pointed like a pistol at my face.

"You stay away from here! And what are you doing to this poor creature?" Hector rushes up to her and wags his tail desperately.

"I'm going to kill Fairy Tale Dora and my little dog too," I tell her, snatching back the leash. Back at the sweet gum, a small crowd has gathered to study Hector's gift to the town. Some are absorbed in the sight like paleontologists unearthing a fossil. The others are glowering at me. They concern me more than Medusa. In Southampton, the crime of not cleaning up after one's dog makes pedophilia look like a misdemeanor. I really need to get home.

Traffic is supposed to stop for pedestrians at the crosswalk, so I pay no attention to the approaching cars as Hector starts to lead us to the far side of Main Street, where we will catch the bus back to Quogue. He trots along with a merry gait. Nothing seems to bother him for long; I don't know whether it's because dogs have short memories or if it's simply the way he is.

Out of the corner of my eye I glimpse an apple-green Rolls-Royce Corniche convertible heading toward us. Something tells me that it is not going to stop at the crosswalk, and I am soon proved right. Hurriedly I yank Hector's leash and pull him out of the way of the careless automobile. As I do, its right front tire clips my right big toe.

So shocked am I by this illegal discourtesy that I do not yelp, though a sharp pain shoots up my leg. Even Hector is taken aback. "Did you see that?" he cries. "I could have been killed!"

Despite my horror of making a spectacle of myself, I fall to the ground and lie there on my side in the middle of the street, glaring after the hit-and-run. I can see only the back of a man's very large head on the driver's side of the convertible. He is wearing one of those wide-brimmed straw plantation owners' hats, and he never even looks over his shoulder to see what he has done. I note the rear license tag, a vanity plate. It reads APHMS.

The policewoman who earlier conferred with Medusa hustles over to where I am lying to ask grimly if I am all right. She looks as frolicsome as a catcher on an all-girls' professional softball team, and young enough to have received her badge and uniform on the same day as her First Communion. A crowd of six or seven coalesces, then disperses. A nun wearing aviator sunglasses reaches down to press a dollar into my hand. "Poor man," she says. I pull myself up, refusing the officer's help. Naturally, she did not see what happened and knows only that I fell in the street. I assume she thinks I am looped.

"Was that who I think it was?" asks Hector, staring after Lapham's Rolls as though it were a chunk of roast beef on wheels.

The policewoman insists that I be checked at Southampton Hospital, a few blocks away. I try to protest that I'm perfectly OK, but my limp betrays me. She half ushers, half pushes me and Hector into the backseat of her patrol car.

"I wasn't askin'," she says. "And by the way, I understand you were behavin' like a creep in the toy store. You're lucky I'm only takin' you to the hospital."

I grasp my toe and feel it throb. "Hector! You're the bomb!" someone calls from the street.

"That's me, all right," I tell the policewoman. "Lucky."

Thirteen

Is it you?" She studies my face in her rearview mirror, through the black wire mesh that separates her seat from the one reserved for us child molesters. I flinch. The siren splits open my head, exposes my brain, then commences drilling. Hector sits beside me in the New York Public Library lion position. The toe begins to bulge out of my Teva like a quick-ripening plum.

"Yes." I am more certain of my answer than of her meaning.

"I had you in high school," she says. I do not bother to offer a cute reply. "We were made to read one of your stories. It was about a couple who had sex during a wake. I didn't get it. You still writin'?"

"No, I'm boning up for the Police Academy."

"Yeah. Funny." She turns off Main Street toward the hospital.

"This is ridiculous. Just let me off anywhere. Thanks very much."

"It wasn't me lyin' in the middle of Main Street holdin' my toe. This is for your own good." She turns to me. "And this is for mine." She reaches back through a small window in the wire mesh and hands me a ticket for Hector's dump. I hand it to Hector, who bites it.

"Is the siren really necessary?"

"You don't want the siren? No siren." She turns the thing off.

"I like the siren," Hector says to me. Now he is up on his hind legs, his front paws braced against the left rear window. I check the hour. Five o'clock approaches. "I *love* the siren," he corrects himself.

"Too bad you can't make your wishes known to the nice police officer."

"I'm praying for you," he says. "You can never tell how serious a toe injury might be. The poor crushed little fellow might shoot a blood clot straight up a vein into your heart, in which case you'll die in a matter of seconds. You'll be gone. Then what?" He pretends to weep. "What will happen to poor little Hector then? Where will he go? A foster home? An orphanage? The North Shore Animal League? And how long will little Hector be kept alive there, with no nice family to come along and see him whooping up the wood chips and fall in love with him on the spot? How long before little Hector is deemed expendable, and they use that euphemism about 'sleep'? Oh . . ." Now he is keening. "Oh, is there no one on this great wide earth who will rescue little Hector?"

I am grateful when we pull into the emergency entrance. Hector adopts his Save-My-Master tilt. An orderly or whatever they are called these days—a physician's mobile assistant—trots out to the driveway to meet us. I crawl out of the police car, refuse his help, and drag my wounded foot toward the door.

"Don't thank me," says the policewoman, who is standing by her car, arms folded in front of her. "I was just doin' my duty."

"In the time you've wasted on me, you could have caught two serial killers and an arsonist."

"I'd have preferred their company." Hector finds her hilarious. She gets back into the driver's seat, puts the patrol car in gear, and begins to pull away. "And stay out of toy stores," she calls.

"You're a doll." I wave good-bye.

"No dogs in the E.R.," says the orderly.

"Where I go, he goes." I repress a sigh. "This is a waste of time," I inform him. "Entirely unnecessary."

The orderly takes down some basic information, fills out a form, then insists that I climb onto a gurney to take the weight off my toe. A doctor will look me over shortly, he assures me. It had *better* be shortly. He reaches into his pocket and produces a Band-Aid with a yellow smiley face on it. "Sorry," he says. "It's all I have." My toe smiles up at me.

Later and later. If I fail to find some usable material . . . "Say, you don't happen to keep any horsehair around the hospital, do you?" He regards me clinically, as if wondering if he has made too superficial a diagnosis. His eyes loiter on my bandaged ear.

"O Lord," Hector begins to pray, "I come to You on bended knee in spirit because, as You know, I am unable to bend my knees, and still I come to beg You for the life of my master. Make him whole again, O Lord. Heal him in mind and in toe, so that he will abandon his bootless acrimony and pursue a life of virtue and quietude, from now on and evermore, attending faithfully to his little Westie, Thy servant, Hector. Amen."

"Beautiful," I tell him. "Inspiring." He howls a gratingly sharp version of "How Great Thou Art."

Ten minutes pass, then twelve. Flat on my back, I can see only the ceiling, which I am persuaded is lowering toward me. On a table beside the gurney sits a stack of publications by area authors: *A Celebrity Guide to the Hamptons (With Addresses and Phone Numbers)*; *Hedges I Have Known*; *Baking Halibut for Fifty*; a coffee-table book of photographs of sunglasses and lip balm; and a copy of *Envy*, a glossy magazine with pictures of movie stars who live in the Hamptons attending the East Hampton premiere of *Love Hamptons Style*, in which they make cameo appearances.

The toe hurts, but not so badly as to prevent me from hoisting myself up onto my forearms and elbows. I have to get out of here. Stealthily, I inch toward the edge of the gurney.

"Is it you?" A whiny male voice is aimed at my head. Suddenly I am looking up into the lemon face of Dr. Whatshisname, of Sag Harbor, by whom I have been accosted before. "It *is* you!" he says. "This is great." He must be referring to my hospitalization. "I was thinking of you only this morning."

"Why was that? And while you're telling me, could you give me a hand and help me off this contraption?"

"You all right?"

"Sure. I came in after an attack of persiflage, but I'm cured."

"You're lucky," he says, not listening to a syllable. "My acid reflux gets worse every day. I come here twice a week. Had a terrible bout today, which is why I was thinking of you." I won't ask, but it will make no difference. "I got another rejection. That's five this month. Can you beat that?"

Regrettably, I know what he is talking about. Whatshisname used to be a nip-and-tuck plastic surgeon in New York, but he lost all his patients because he forced them to listen to him read excerpts from his unpublished novels before they went under the knife. In fact, after hearing him read, several patients walked out, deciding that they liked their original looks after all. He then moved to Sag Harbor, where he committed himself to his art full-time. When his efforts were rejected by every mainstream house in New York, he became a self-publisher. He writes to me every so often to complain of this outrage, which he terms a conspiracy, and to ask if I will intercede on his behalf. I tried to pass him off to Vandersnook, but the great man wanted to charge Whatshisname a fee for the service.

"Don't worry," I tell him, as I do every time. "I'm on the case."

"And while you're at it," he says as he helps me to my feet, "see if you can find out why I am not invited to speak at writers gatherings around here. Why am I forced to give readings on my own sunporch? Is that fair?"

"Another outrage," I assure him.

"You bet your ass it is." He hugs me, and in doing so steps on my injured toe. I groan. "That's the spirit," he says, and he departs, leaving me clinging to the gurney for balance.

"I like him," says Hector.

I transfer my weight to my working foot, pull myself back up, and wait for the renewed pain to subside. I wonder when the real doctor will appear and if he will turn out to be Lapham himself, ready to anesthetize me with his conversation, then operate and remove both my legs. From my lower depths, I hear, "Is it you?"

This time the question is asked by a woman whom I do not recognize. A cloud of white hair encircles a face so fiercely coy that it appears to be peeking out from itself. "Yes!" she exults. "It *is* you!" She introduces herself as the chairperson of the benefit committee for the Endangered Turtles Ball, a perennial gala held for and by the slow.

"We've been trying to contact you all summer"—her tone wavering between delirium and emergency. She clings to her vowels. "And here you are! On the very same day I'm conferring with Dr. Brouhaha, another committee member. Wait till I tell him that I saw you right here in the hospital. It's destiny!"

"God's will," Hector whispers.

"Well!" she exhales, as if the word constituted the entirety of a conversation. She is a coliseum of merriment. "Well! Here's what we've been wanting to ask you." Hector, imitating her hopped-up fervor, wags his tail wildly and tosses her the rescue-me look. "What a charming dog!" she says. "What's her name?"

"Hermione."

He growls.

"Well! All of us on the committee would be thrilled if you would lend your name to the ball this year. Thrilled! You wouldn't have to actually *do* anything, of course. We're asking for contributions of one thousand dollars each from 'House Pet Turtles' and twenty-five thousand from 'Golden Turtles.' It would mean so much if we could add you to our list."

"Sorry," I tell her. "My religious convictions prohibit it. And then there are the dietary laws." She seems confused, though she says she understands perfectly.

"Well!" she says again, her voice not flagging. "As long as I have you here, Mr. March, I wonder if you might glance at the manuscript of my first novel." She reaches into her tote bag, which has a weeping turtle painted on the side, and under it the words "Save Me." "It's about a woman who lives in Water Mill, as I do, who comes upon a turtle named Sweetie on the beach near her home. Sweetie is dying, but the woman nurses her back to health, and the two of them become great friends and have many adventures together. Would you read it? I'd be thrilled!"

"No."

"Well! I also have my husband's first novel with me." She is not kidding. "It's about a rat named Ebola who escapes from Plum Island and swims all the way to Water Mill, where he causes the horrible deaths of all the women in town. Would you read it? He'd be thrilled!"

"No."

"Well, take this little darling anyway," she says. She reaches into her bag again and pulls out a fuzzy toy turtle the size of a deflated football that she thrusts into my arms. It wears a pink tam-o'-shanter and has a satin teardrop sewn beneath its right eye. When I give it a squeeze, its tiny voice pleads, "Save me."

"It must be wonderful," says Hector as the woman departs in a hailstorm of hand waves. "It must be wonderful, the literary life. To be a literary lion, as you are. I'm a literary dog, you know." I look away. "Oh yes. Our church library has an event every year to honor the literary lights, mostly dogs who write how-to books and celebrity autobiographies. It's quite a night!"

"I'm sure it is."

"Is Mr. Lapham a literary lion?" he asks.

"Definitely."

"He has an awfully nice car. Do you suppose he might give me a ride someday? He must miss his dear departed Westie."

A TV monitor is broadcasting the news, giving me no choice but to listen. "And from our culture corner," a frantic young man is announcing, "that great old series *Murder She Wrote* is completely going off the air. They finally ran out of repeats, Charlie. Back to you."

To his credit, and my surprise, Hector says nothing.

"Excuse me," I call to a woman passing my gurney. "Do you suppose you could help me off this thing?"

"Is it you?" she says. I acknowledge the local gossip reporter, Parrot Light, so nicknamed because she reports anything anyone tells her. She has the face of Natalie Wood, though without the dolorous depth. In the 1980s she worked as a correspondent in the Middle East but was dismissed after filing a story in which she revealed that Yasir Arafat was preparing to drive every last Israeli into the sea. Arafat's third in command had told her so himself.

"Sure," she says, extending her hand. I sit up, stare, and wait for the only question she ever asks me.

"Because I ran out of Bic pens," I tell her this time. She jots that down.

"All of them?"

"That's a follow-up question." I pat her on the head and move toward the door.

"Oh, Mr. March," Parrot calls after me. "I've always wondered, where do you live?"

"On Noman," I am able to say at long last, a tremor of small satisfaction hovering on my horizon. She asks what I know she will ask. "Noman is an island," I inform her, and I await her reaction.

"Oh. OK," she says. She makes a note to herself and walks off.

"We're out of here," I say to Hector, and we are but a few feet from freedom.

"Is it you?"

I turn to face a young man with copper-colored hair, wearing blue-and-green scrubs. He looks like a lollipop. "You're not leaving, are you? I haven't examined your toe yet."

"I'm fine," I promise him. "Thanks all the same. But I really must get home now."

"I ought to take a look, just to be on the safe side. We don't want to lose a citizen like Harry March to a damaged toe." He hacks up a laugh and forcibly guides me back to the gurney. "You know," he says, in enough of a drawl to suggest that what is about to follow is going to be horrendous. "You know, I'm something of a writer myself." Hector looks up at him, feigning avid interest. "Of course, I'm not a writer the way *you're* a writer. But I know I have a book in me." I do not say, Why don't you leave it there? "A book about my life as a Southampton physician."

"Is that so?" I find myself missing Whatshisname, Light, and Mrs. Turtle. He squeezes my toe to see if it hurts.

"Yes. I'm going to call it *Hamptons M.D.: The Life of a Country Doctor*."

"Fantastic title," I tell him. "But I must be off."

"You wouldn't believe the stories."

"I'd love to hear them," Hector says.

"I'd love to hear them," I say to the doctor. "But I must get back to my wife. She swore she'd turn to stone if I wasn't home in time to help her with our dinner party."

"Tell me about it!" he says. I do not. "Nothing broken. So off you go. But try to stay off that toe."

As we are about to exit the E.R., Medusa is wheeled in on a gurney of her own. "She's hyperventilating," explains the orderly who earlier put the smile on my toe. "A pervert attacked her in her store." I attempt to avert my existence, without success.

"Is it you?" she shrieks, then points to the toy turtle still in my grip. "Oh my God!" She rolls on.

Reflexively, I go to fling the thing into a trash can, but the woman from the Endangered Turtles Ball, still chatting in the lobby, catches me in the act. "Well!" She glowers at me, then rushes to retrieve the discarded mascot, wipes it off, and pats its tam. The turtle bleats, "Save me."

Out on the street at last, I signal for a taxi. Hector jumps in, and I crawl in behind him, using my forearms for leverage. Like all Hamptons taxi drivers, this one weighs four hundred pounds and appears to be permanently wedged into his vehicle. His belly tapers up to a pair of boy-size shoulders, like a Buddha's. I tell him we're going to Quogue.

"Is it you?" he asks. "You know, I'm doing a book that might interest you, about the secret roads and byways of the

Hamptons. It'll be a real time-saver for motorists. I'm calling it *The Road Less Traveled*. What do you think?"

"Me too," Hector says softly. "I'm writing a book called *The Cat in the Manger*. It's a religious book about a bruiser of a Persian who refuses to let the Wise Men near the baby Jesus. I've already sold it to the movies. Mary is going to be played by Glenn Close, Joseph by Anthony Hopkins, Jesus by the latest Culkin boy, and the cat by Garfield. And for Peter the Apostle, I'd like to get that handsome young British actor who starred in *Four Weddings and a Funeral* and so many other sprightly comedies. You know who I mean—Grant. Fabulous actor. Grant. Can't think of his first name. Is it Hugh?"

Fourteen

The only sensible thing for me to do now is chop down the walls of my house. So, upon returning home, I am bound to do just that. No time to hesitate, no time for anything but action. Odd, is it not? Whoever invented time did not want things to happen all at once, and yet they do. At this moment, as the Chautauquans are whipping themselves into a frenzy of anticipation of my visit, at the same time, in the same world, Lapham is addressing himself in a full-length mirror in an effort to determine whether he looks senatorial, Hector is scratching the back of his head with his left hind paw, and I, checking the time, note that it is not on my side.

Yet barely have I placed my Oedipal foot on my beach when a young female voice cries to me out of the mist. "I need to sell you a swimming pool." A girl in a kayak swoops inside the *L* of the dock, like a gull.

"What are you talking about?" I attempt to shoo her away.

"A swimming pool," she chirps. She ties up to my rowboat, strides toward me, and eases herself into the Adirondack chair. Naturally, Hector sidles up to her, his tail as agitated as his useless penis.

"He loves me," says the girl.

"He loves everyone but me," I tell her.

"He's precious."

She is twenty, I suppose, though these days I can barely tell a twenty-year-old girl from a fifty-year-old woman. This one has an Irish look, her longish black hair parted on the left side, the way Gene Tierney's was in *Laura*. Her body is longish too, slim and neat in a yellow one-piece bathing suit that contrasts attractively with the forest green of the chair. Her skin is pearly. She smells of biscuits.

"I'll give you two minutes." I slump into the chaise and face her.

And all at once I realize that I was wrong about Pam, the waitress who brought me blueberry pancakes topped with vanilla ice cream at the Hampton Bays Diner last month; wrong about the girl in Bookhampton whose neck showed seashell white as she bent over a volume of Terence; wrong about the redhead in the Miata, and about the one in the shampoo ad on TV during *Murder She Wrote*. *This* is the girl. This is the girl I ought to be with forever. The one with whom I should live out my remaining years, playing Chopin on the pianoforte while making exquisite puns at tea. Then she opens her mouth.

"Mr. March, everyone around here says I could never sell you one of my dad's pools. My dad says so too. Everyone says you're mean and crazy as all get-out."

"They're right. So get out."

The time is six o'clock on the dot. I really am up against it.

She backhands the air as if scattering gnats. "But I said, No, that old man is just waiting for a little brightness in his life."

"In the form of a swimming pool?"

"You said it!" She reaches toward the chaise and clasps my hand in both of hers, as if we were at a political convention. "What you need to cheer up your cranky and miserable life is a new Gunite pool with a Stanford-Cox filtration system, a Kolbell pump—they last forever—a Levinthal heater, which makes even the coldest December day feel toasty, and Newman stone and tile landscaping, all installed with expert craftsmanship and tender loving care by the czar of Hamptons pool makers and servicers, Tony Alvarez."

"Your father." I find myself looking for her baby teeth.

"My father." She reaches into the top of her bathing suit and pulls out a business card, as if conjuring a magic trick. "Anthony's Aqua Heaven. Pools and Service. Night and Day."

" 'You are the one,' " I mutter.

" 'Only you beneath the moon or under the sun.' " She

sings the line rather well and extends her long legs toward me. Her toenails are fire-engine red.

"Good going, señor!" comes the cry across the creek from Little Mexico. "We see that you took our advice!" They whistle, clap, and cheer. "But she looks a leetle old for you!"

"She's trying to sell me a swimming pool," I call to José.

"A girl like that could sell me the moon!" She gives him a friendly wave. "Buy it, señor! I would if I had the money—if I had the money to buy anything." He laughs. Dave orders his men back to work.

I turn back to her. "Miss, I have important things to do. I have no need of or any desire for a swimming pool. I have no one to impress. If I want to swim, I do it off my dock. If I want the water warm, I take a bath."

"Good for you! But I must tell you, I don't think you're seeing this issue clearly." She taps my knee like a schoolmarm. "You are thinking of a swimming pool narrowly, as a place to exercise or loll about. And speaking of exercise, if you don't mind my saying so, you could use some."

"I *do* mind. Your two minutes are up."

She settles deeper into the Adirondack chair. "Think of a swimming pool instead as another notable room of your house." She glances at my house and mutely ascertains that it has no notable rooms. She should see it after I go at it with my ax. "Think of it as your indoor body of water, your pond, your lake, your estuary. What, may I ask, is more beautiful than a body of water? The light dance of the ripples, the shadows on the waves, the brooding darkness underneath?"

I consider giving her a mini-sermon on the effect of swimming pools on the American soul, a history that begins with the public's first glimpses of the things in the private duchies of Hollywood actors and their scrawny nymphets; winds through the turquoise oases of streamlined motels, with inflated pink sea serpents squashed beneath the asses of Finnair hostesses and discontented mothers of five; reaches its zenith in the bright and lurid satires of David Hockney; and culminates in the oblong "inground" holes of every community with a marina or a links. Fly over the Republic, I could urge her, and take stock of the pockmarked map of languid blue rectangles and kidneys that outnumber the fields of corn and wheat and malting barley. And then tell me again how everyone needs a pool. But I refrain.

For a different perspective, I could also relate the story of the drunken American Studies professor who, one night a few summers back, hoped to re-create Cheever's "The Swimmer" by doing a medley of strokes in a series of private pools in East Hampton. He made it safely into and out of three estates but was shot in midbutterfly attempting the fourth. In a way, though, I have to admit, that anecdote only reinforces her sales pitch.

The girl may be overdoing it, but she is no dope. I tell her so in guarded terms and ask why she is wasting what is obviously a first-class mind on selling swimming pools, filial piety aside.

"But it never is 'aside.' My dad is having a hard time of it this summer. I mean, moneywise."

"Moneywise'?" I clamp my hands over my ears, reviving the pain in one of them. "Please! Is this your full-time occupation?"

"Summerwise," she says, with just enough of a smile to signal that she realizes she has milked the joke dry and will not try it again. "Then it's back to St. John's in Annapolis."

"The Great Books curriculum!" I say too enthusiastically. "I thought so! You're an anachronism."

"Just like you."

"Yes, but I've earned that status. You're much too young."

"Maybe. But it looks better on me." She shoots me an are-you-smiling? look. "When I was in high school, I had a clear choice of extracurricular activities: be an anachronism—spend time at old movies, listen to jazz, live in the library—or give blow jobs to the doped-up future actuaries of America."

I laugh out loud.

"So I went to classes most of the day and lived at the town library most of the night." She sees that I am interested.

"Sure you don't want to buy a swimming pool? It's a great investment. Well," she continues, "I got fixated on Samuel Johnson." My gasp is audible. "First I read Boswell. Then I read the great doctor himself: *Lives of the Poets*. The dictionary. The poems. The best of which is . . ."

"*The Vanity of Human Wishes*," we say in unison. This is a very strange moment, even in a day filled with strange moments. I find myself, against all odds and inclinations, pleased to be engaged in conversation, even with time running out. And a conversation with whom? A girl barely out of her teens. But she knows *The Vanity of Human Wishes*. She knows how good it is. And she got there by herself. My wicked nature smells a Southern rat. Did the conniving Polite send over a Lorelei who is pretending to know Dr. Johnson and his works in order to set me up? I decide to test her. In the middle of whatever she is saying, I interrupt. " 'When a man is tired of London . . .' "

" '. . . he is tired of life,' " she finishes the quotation.

I trot out my favorite: " 'Is not a patron, my lord, one who looks with unconcern on a man struggling for life in the water . . .' "

" '. . . and when he has reached the ground encumbers him with help?' "

Hector grumbles, "Brilliant!"

She frowns. "Either make them difficult or don't play at all."

Sink me, as the Scarlet Pimpernel used to say, I'm floored. She's the genuine article. "What brought you to Dr. Johnson?" I ask.

She looks out over the creek. "First it was his devotion to the power of reason: 'How rare reason guides the stubborn choice.' But what sealed it was the lovely sweetness of the man. I wish I'd been Boswell. I would have recorded more of the sweetness and fewer of the wisecracks." She adds, "And he was always right."

"You are more than an anachronism, young lady. You show real value." From the far shore erupts another volley of bangs. *Bang bang bang.* "Not like that monster over there," I add.

"Lapham?"

"You know him? You've seen him?"

"No. I don't know anyone who's seen him. 'He is one of the many . . .'"

I cannot believe she knows this quotation. I complete it: "'. . . one of the many who have made themselves public without making themselves known.'" She merely *hmmm*s. Then she turns to me and says earnestly, "I wouldn't worry about him if I were you. I'd look to thyself."

"What do you know about me?" I ask.

"What I see. What others say. But mainly what I see. A man

who has whittled his life to too fine a point. Too brittle. A man who used to do good work when he opened up, when he wasn't playing it safe. But that was a long time ago. Now he doesn't write anymore. Now he is reduced to the stupidity of a sage."

" 'Towering in the confidence of twenty-one,' " I quote again.

A sulk flits across the lower half of her face, then gives way to aggression. "An answer for everything," she says with a note of disgust. But now she softens her gaze. "I don't want to fight with you. Besides, there's something morally wrong about quarreling when we're speaking of a man we both love." No argument from me. Just when I was adamantly certain that I had condemned the race accurately, justifiably, and universally, an exception to the rule paddles up in a kayak.

"It's the selflessness of the poem," she is saying of *The Vanity*. That's what gets to me. It's what thrills me about all of Dr. Johnson. The certain knowledge of how weak and puny we are, all of us struggling little creatures. And yet beautiful too, for the very fact of our struggling. Because life is so hard, you know?" I do know, but how does she?

We sit saying nothing for a while. I feel the urge to confide something to her—anything at all—but I resist, because confidences invariably lead to trouble. She looks at her watch. "Well," she says finally, the tone of her voice rising. "How about it?" From her bathing suit she extracts a contract and a ballpoint pen. As she hands them to me, she grazes the tips of my fingers with her own. Her eyes claim mine. *Bang bang bang bang bang.* Now I too am awakened from the trance, and my eyes scan the terms of the contract. "Three installments," she says. Gaah. At least she did not say "easy installments."

"Do you remember this from the opening of *The Vanity?*" I ask her. " 'Wealth heaped on wealth, nor truth nor safety buys, / The dangers gather as the treasures rise.' "

She nods. "And the import of that?" she asks.

"A swimming pool is a luxury. I do not want luxury. 'Life is a progress from want to want,' " I quote again, " 'not from enjoyment to enjoyment.' "

"That's just Dr. Johnson being moody," she says. "Nobody believes that. The trouble with you is that you don't really understand him at all. You think he was simply a font of wisdom and not a man. Dr. Johnson was *poor*, dirt-poor. He thought like a poor man, like my father. He thought like Tony Alvarez."

"He would not have rowed around the Thames selling swimming pools," I tell her. "He would have sold dictionaries."

She stands and brushes the sand from her bathing suit.

"You never know what poor people will do," she says coldly, and walks toward her kayak, kicking and splashing.

"Are you coming back?" Why do I ask? Soon there may be no *back* for her to come to.

"Are you buying a pool?" She does not expect an answer. I watch her climb in, push off, and slice into the creek, where she disappears part by part into the lowering white fog.

"She is wrong," I say aloud. Johnson would never have contaminated his principles for a few pennies. I could go after her. That's the way it's done, is it not? I could go after her, catch up, leap from my rowboat into her kayak, make an endearing remark about our being in the same boat, and hold her to me forever—against all propriety, against common sense and logic, against all the forces of the material world, except, of course, swimming pools.

And then she does turn, violently, to face me. Her expression is a verdict—severe, and dissolving any advantage I might have enjoyed for being so much older and in the right. "You are not an eighteenth-century man, by the way," she calls to me. "I thought you'd like to know."

"What do you mean?" I ask.

"You're a Romantic," she says. She might as well have chucked a spear through my body. "You live on an island," she goes on. "You create your own ideal world. You despise or ignore the real world. You belittle life as it is. And you feel superior to others. What do you suppose that makes you?"

"Lonely," I tell her.

She casts me a look somewhere between pity and reproach, but closer to pity, I think. I am too preoccupied to make certain. I have no need or will to hang on to the image of this girl. I ought to regret that more than I do.

Fifteen

At 6:19, it is do or die. Hector follows me to the cord of wood I keep stacked off to the side of the porch. He is half alarmed, half amused.

"You know," he says as he watches me hobble, "you are beginning to look very much like a pirate. A buccaneer. And if you don't mind my saying so, a mighty handsome one at that. Yes. There's no denying it: that limp, that bandaged ear, that scowl—all very swashbuckling, whatever that means, Captain. And I'll be your colorful pet, if you will allow me. I shall perch upon your shoulder and repeat all the very clever things you say."

"Why don't you try it?"

Bang bang bang bang bang. The industrious Mexicans do not skip a beat. They do not give up, and neither will I. As they construct to destroy, so will I destroy to construct. Up goes one wall, down comes another. But which wall should get the ax? The one in the parlor, I think. It is the widest in the house and therefore, it stands to reason, must have required the greatest amount of horsehair when it was built. I commend my mind on its ability to render cool analysis in the throes of frenzy.

Hector backs away. I raise the ax and bring it down. The wall crumbles like stale cake. I strike again and again, hoping that the span contains no supporting beams. And again. And again. In a twinkling the parlor wall is a dusty pile of its former self.

"Well done!" says Hector.

Using both hands, I ransack a portion of the plaster. Nothing. Another portion. Still nothing. A third.

"Here," says Hector. "Let me help." He gallops back and forth through the plaster in a mocking imitation of my own frantic behavior, generating a small blizzard into which his whiteness disappears. "No horsehair?" he exclaims. "No horsehair in the wall? What can have happened back in the eighteen twenties? Did the house builders run out of horses? Did the horses go on strike? Or did the horses build the house themselves and not wish to sacrifice their coats? Oh, well. Let's not accept defeat so easily. There are plenty of walls around here—let's chop 'em all down. Wait, I know! The horsehair is in the ceiling! They probably used jumpers like Mr. Huey!"

Suddenly he turns toward the creek. "It's Dave," he says. "Come to help us chop down the house. We're saved! Thank you, Jesus!"

Dave it is. What now? Whatever it is he wants, it shouldn't take long. A creature of habit, he will pull up on the outside of the dock without tying the boat, cut the engine, tell me what he has to tell me, and go away. I limp in a jerky lope down to where the dock angles left, the covered Da Vinci at my side.

"What are you doing, Harry?"

"Doing?" I must look about as innocent as Hector did when I questioned him about the horsehair.

"All that banging."

"Surely a little banging wouldn't disturb you."

"I didn't want to say this in front of the men"—he has chosen to ignore my meager attempt to go on the offensive—"but I know you're up to something." His tone is a mixture of worry and warning.

"How do you know?" My question concedes the fact.

"That ax, for starters." I didn't realize I was still holding on to it. "And the stuff you had delivered by those FedEx barges. I don't know what that junk is, but it looks fishy." He indicates the tarp. "And look at you. What is that, plaster?" I see what he means. I look like Jacob Marley fresh from the grave.

"Oh, it's nothing, just a little project of mine. I'm making a collectible bust of John Dryden. So no one will forget him."

"Are you planning to do something stupid?" I tilt my head and try to affect Hector's expression of offended shock, but again he ignores me. "You're behaving very strangely, even for you. You don't write anymore. That hole in your shirt. Those notes to Lapham's man every day. That toy boat. The statue of your wife. Your ear. And now you're limping, aren't you?" If he goes over the complete list, I'll be here for a week.

"And you talk to *him*." Hector wags happily at his inclusion. Dave breaks into a tolerant smile and cracks, "At least he doesn't talk back." Hector rolls over for the first time in his life in what appears to be a laughing fit. "You all right, Harry?" Dave asks.

"Right as rain." I point to the threatening sky. If there were a last man on earth to whom I would confess my plot, other than Lapham himself, it would be Dave. He is one of those few who always know and do the right thing, the sort of fellow civilizations depend upon for continuity, and thus, to me, dangerous.

"You know," he says, "I'm sorry about all the hammering, and about that air conditioner." He has changed his tack to sweet reason, the way one does with children and the mad. "But we have to get this job finished on time."

I tell him that I understand perfectly, but my graciousness and sudden affability put him on guard. Fortunately, he thinks I am merely upset about the noise.

"In a couple of weeks we'll be out of your hair." I summon a vision of the head of Kathy Polite detached.

"Perhaps sooner," I tell him, and immediately wish I could take it back. I try to convey simple optimism: "Don't bother about me."

"How'd things go in Southampton, by the way?" he asks.

"Smooth as silk."

He frowns at my cheer. "You *are* up to something."

"Where's Jack going to college?" I ask him, desperate to change the subject. Mention a good man's child, and you'll get his attention.

"That's a sore point. He got into NYU on early admission, but I can't afford to send him. He's too good a kid to complain. If I had the money, I'd give it to him." He shrugs. "But a fact's a fact."

"A fact is a fact" is precisely the reason I like Dave. In his own straight-shooter way, he is my eighteenth-century man: protects his family, does his work, pays his way, lives on the earth like any other animal. Should I take him with me to Chautauqua as a living exhibit of my thesis? I'd suggest it to him just to see his reaction.

And I like Jack. When he isn't helping his father or doing valet parking for people like the Bittermans, he works at Westhampton Hardware on Montauk Highway. He has done so since he was twelve, supplementing his father's income and pulling his own weight, which is one of the reasons he'll be starting university at twenty-one rather than eighteen. He's honest and honorable, like his old man, with the same backbone. He once told me that his favorite movie was *The Maltese Falcon*, and when I asked him why, he said it was because at the end, "Sam Spade does the right thing because he doesn't want to." For a kid, he is also a modern oddball insofar as he does not think the world was created with him in mind. Jack will be the first one in Dave's family to go to college.

"So where is he headed instead?" I ask.

"Stony Brook. Which is a perfectly good place. It just doesn't have a film school."

"That's what Jack wants to do?"

Dave nods and looks at the water. This is the first time in all the years I have known him that he has seemed downcast, and it is just for an instant. He is not embarrassed that I caught him in the act. He is embarrassed by the act. "It's no big deal," he says.

"Wait here a minute." I raise my hand, palm outstretched in the time-out signal, limp back up the beach, and head into the house. The Money Room smells like wet leaves; it has been that long since I last set foot in it. I grab some stacks of hundreds—I figure maybe twenty-five thousand dollars, give or take—stuff them into a garbage bag, tie it at the top in a nice gift bow, and return to the dock. I toss Dave the bag. I am a very accurate tosser.

He gives me a what's-this? look, unties the bow, sticks his face in the bag, and comes out blinking like Fairy Tale Dora. Then he asks directly, "What's this?"

"A bribe. A down payment for your work stoppage on Lapham's house. Play your cards right, and there'll be more where that came from. Thanks."

"But I haven't agreed to stop work on Lapham's house," he says. "And I don't take bribes."

I am tickled that he ever takes me seriously. "OK, if that's the way you want it." I try to sound defeated. "Then use it for Jack, to make up the difference between Stony Brook's tuition and NYU's."

"I can't do that."

I move away back up the dock so that he won't be able to lob the bag to me without risking losing it in the creek. He tries to lasso a piling so as to pull his boat toward me, but I kick the rope back with my one good leg. This is my first moment of fun today, but it is no fun for Dave. "I can't take this money," he says, as definite as he should be.

"It's not for you, it's for Jack. Let him know it's a business transaction, grown-up to grown-up. He's ready for this." I ought to be ashamed at how easy it is for me to find the best tactic to use with him, but I'm not. "Tell Jack this is a loan from me to him, man-to-man, and that I expect him to repay me with the profits he makes from his first film, which had better be no higher than the amount of the loan. That way it'll be guaranteed to be a worthwhile work of art."

Dave studies the contents of the bag as though the money might change into coal at any second. "You're not kidding?" he says. We have known each other long enough, in that type of silent, comradely friendship that men prefer, for him to take no offense. I am counting on that. I nod as a New Englander might in greeting. He actually scratches his head. "I'll think about it," he says, and gently places the bag in the hold as though he were setting down a baby bird.

"You do that," I tell him.

"You *are* nuts." His face shows a suggestion of relief worth a good twenty-five thousand dollars. For my part, I am even more relieved than he is, since he seems to have forgotten what it was he came over for.

"Thank you. Jack is very talented. His mother says so."

"Got to go," I say. "Busy, busy." Then I turn. "Oh, Dave? One more thing. Don't tell Jack about this till you get home." I do not wish to talk about money, and I definitely do not want the boy coming over to thank me. Any more visitors this evening, and I'm cooked. I may be cooked anyway: no horsehair, no torsion spring, no Da Vinci, no Chautauqua, no me.

"Well!" says Hector as we start back to the house.

"What's the matter with you?"

"What's the matter with *me*? You can afford to send Dave's boy to college, but you won't send me to business school? Me, your constant companion. Me, who has provided you with affection and interesting conversation and religious instruction, and who has been at your side for over sixty-three years. Sixty-three years! I'll bet Mr. Lapham gave his Westie whatever he wanted."

"Will you ever shut up?"

"When the time comes."

Sixteen

It is now 6:48. Across the creek, Kathy alights from her cream-colored Mercedes and catches sight of me sitting in a despondent slump on my porch rocking chair. As ever, she is the last person I wish to see (at least at this hour), yet also the one I need. She flashes me a wave that combines a piano finger exercise with the Hitler salute. I do not salute back. A yellow Hummer pulls up, and out slithers a designer-thin middle-aged couple in pressed jeans. They are as stiff as pithed frogs. Kathy exclaims, "Fab, isn't it?" as she presents the half-completed Attica nearest Lapham's. He says yes. She says yes.

Kathy watches me watching her. She flips her braid like a horse's tail in my direction, and I wince. After her clients depart—exclaiming, "Well, you certainly have given us a lot to think about!"—she stands on the shore with legs apart, cups her hands to her mouth like a hog caller, and hollers: "Going-out-of-business sale! One day only!" Her voice is so shrill she has no need of the bullhorn.

"Last chance, Wrinkles! Here comes the countdown!"

I glide in a dream state and run what's left of my mind over the events of the summer so far.

At the start of the season, on Memorial Day, a dual funeral was held in Wainscott for two women who were killed fighting over a salmon steak. It seems that the salmon was the only one left in the seafood shop after the weekend run, and both women had entered the shop at the same time. They raced over and grabbed the piece of fish, each hanging on to one slippery end as best she could, but their tug-of-war carried them out to the terrace of the shop. There they tumbled over the railing and into a truck loaded with shrimp, in which they suffocated to death before anyone could reach them.

When I read of this, I wondered if, at the funeral, the women had been laid out on beds of lettuce with cocktail sauce on the side, but I failed to inquire.

"Going once . . ."

Last month, the Kerouac Literary Prize, nicknamed the "Roady," was awarded in a Nobel-like ceremony in a field of stiff thistles in the town of Flanders. The Roady is supposed to go to an East End writer of distinction (I once declined it myself, having come down with Tourette's that year), but the selection committee of 207 local watercolorists and poetasters long ago ran out of first-rank candidates, then out of second-rank, then third-, until they began giving away the award to anyone who wrote anything at all. This year's Roady went to Betsy Betsy, a beat reporter over whose selection there was a brief dustup, since Ms. Betsy also chairs the committee of 207. Nonetheless, everyone much admired her columns on media business transactions in *Envy* magazine, and thought her Roady was well deserved. A motion to give the award to everyone on Long Island was tabled.

"Going once-and-a-half . . ."

As August began, Jacob McMinus, the Wall Street mogul who served time for insider trading, threw himself a seventieth birthday-and-parole party at his oceanfront estate in East Hampton. The rumored cost was sixteen million dollars. My invitation must have been mislaid, but I understand that the event was a howling success. Guests waltzed to the string section of the New York Philharmonic and were then treated to a tasteful miniconcert by 'N Synch. Royal Beluga caviar was scooped from hollowed-out softballs (Jake loves the game), and every guest received a goody bag worth thirty thousand dollars, containing ampoules of perfume, quarts of Macallan sixty-year-old single-malt scotch, a gift certificate for a year's worth of Botox treatments, and a CD of Jake telling funny dirty stories at work. At the end of the evening the revelers repaired to the beach, where they divvied up the five-hundred-thousand-dollar cake and drank themselves witless. The host thanked his guests, by whose friendship he said he was humbled, and added that for him, jail had been a "life-affirming experience."

On the very same day, a real estate developer who had the misfortune to live north of the highway, and who, for twenty years, had striven to get his name in the "South o' the Highway" column in *Dan's Paper*, without success, hanged himself from the hoop of his backboard, employing the net. He left a note that read: *"Now* do I make it?" Unfortunately his body, though swaying out of doors in plain sight, was not discovered till five days later by two men from So-Low Waste Management. "We wouldn't have found him ourselves," said Lenny Bisselkorf of Swampscut, "if we hadn't had a scheduled pickup. Who goes up here? No one." The developer's death was noted in the "North o' the Highway" column in *Dan's*, but was given a full paragraph.

"Going twice . . ."

Last Saturday the Paint Stores and Publishers softball game was played in East Hampton. Originally this annual charity event was called the Artists and Writers game. But after a few years, the players on the business side of things outnumbered the artists, so they changed the team names. These folks would themselves be overtaken by the Hollywood people as soon as it became clear that the game had publicity potential for the participants, but the game's new name would stick. In recent years some of the biggest stars in movies have been seen shagging flies and making crowd-pleasing attempts at the hidden-ball trick. So popular and competitive has the game grown, in fact, that several network crews are always on hand, along with at least one documentary filmmaker who sees the event as emblematic. The media were in luck this year, as over twenty "bona fide superstars" showed up, two of whom were tossed out of the game for sliding spikes-up into second, and another, disputing a call, split open the home plate umpire's head with an aluminum bat. None of the injured parties complained. They said it was all for a good cause, though at the time no one could recall what the cause was.

"Going twice and a half . . ."

And then just a few days ago, to round off the summer mummery to date, an auction was held at the Water Mill Center for Self-Help, to raise money for the center to help itself. Among the items up for bid were a barbecue at the Bridgehampton home of Helmut and Greta Lopez, recently of São Paulo and widely thought to be war criminals from Vienna "yet fascinating people"; two nights in any Hampton for a couple from one Hampton who wish to see what another Hampton is like; a tour of the U.N. General Assembly conducted by John Travolta; the broken left taillight from the

Mercedes driven by a famous socialite several years ago when she backed into the crowd waiting to get into a club (expected to fetch in the high six figures); and best of all, "*Your* picture with the Laphams at their fabulous new home in Quogue. And a Lapham Aphm written expressly for *you*."

So it goes, so it will always go. Shadows cast by Lapham's twelve virgin chimneys menace the roof, the walls, the green and perfect lawn, and then the water, where they fracture into kaleidoscopic ghosts. I sink deeper into my rocking chair. I am beginning to feel like a notebook dropped into the creek, my handwriting illegible, my pages drowned.

I look at the Da Vinci, then back at Lapham's house, nearly four stories and growing. The overtime Mexicans are on their overtime evening break. They sit with their backs against Lapham's front wall, pass cans of beer from hand to hand, and snooze. I look at the bulging clouds that have crushed the sun into a dappled line on the horizon, and at the creek on whose churning waters ducks float and bob, and toward the cranberry bogs and the rolling moors and the marshy banks on which the egrets and the cormorants strut, and then back at my home, which represents three generations of quiet purpose and attempted decency and yet is only property, real estate, after all, and then finally into my heart, which drums and asks, *Is you is or is you ain't my baby?*

"Going, going . . ."

"All right," I call to Kathy. "You can have the house."

"And the island?" She is deliberately speaking like a little girl.

"And the island."

And my life. I wonder if I can lure her over here by agreeing to anything, then greet her on the beach with the ax.

The thought occurs that I can always renege, until I see that she is holding a pocket-size tape recorder high in the air and smiling like a dolphin.

"OK, Wrinkles. Here comes the hair." And so saying, she displays a pair of cartoonishly large shears, which she must have brought with her, certain in the knowledge that I would cave. She cuts off her long braid with one clip and holds it aloft, as if it were the head of John the Baptist.

"What now?" I ask.

"Well, Ah know Ah said that Ah would hand over this prize to you mahself. Person to nutcase? But frankly, Mr. March, Ah've been observin' you lately, and you seem to be about to topple off that rocker of yours. No offense. So for safety's sake—*mah* safety, that is—Ah think Ah'll just scoot the braid over to you by boat."

"You're not going to send the Grady White over here without a driver? You'll crash it." She cannot be that eager for this deal.

"Oh my, no, silly—*this* boat!" She holds up *Sharon* and lays the detached braid in its toy hull. I hobble down to the dock, grab the remote, watch the vessel come toward me, and whisper good-bye to my life.

Terrible images present themselves to me, of strangers tramping over Noman, through the rooms of my house; Kathy sweeping her arms around and saying things like "Fab, fabulous, marvy, marvelous, like incredible, like wow"; interested parties making inquiries as to what the previous owner was like, and receiving responses to those inquiries, my name being bandied about by aliens; blueprints being drawn up for changes to the property contemplated by would-be buyers; endless discussions being held regarding the addition of tennis courts, a swimming pool, of course, and a helipad; couples negotiating over the location of the genuine antique jukebox ("We have Eddie Fisher singing 'Oh My Papa!'") and the pool table ("Arthur plays a wicked game of pool"); and all their faces, Kathy's included, lost in moronic reverie.

I try not to, but I cannot help but think of them sorrowfully, all of these people who seek the perfect life and believe that a pool table will put it within their reach. However often I condemn and ridicule them and hope they will boil in their own hot tubs, something in me also wants to comfort them, to put my arm around their exfoliated shoulders and tell them that the pool table, whose green felt now appears as an infinite landscape, soon will feel like an inch-square swath of fabric, as will their lives; that one fine evening, when the din of their schedules has momentarily ceased, and much to their horrified surprise not a single envelope bearing arabesque calligraphy has arrived in the mail, and there is nowhere (nowhere!) for them to go, they will descend to their pool-table room and stare at the soft green rectangle and weep without tears.

Sharon arrives. I extract the braid and unravel it. The hair is just right: strong, heavy, and springy. My triumphs have come to this.

"One question," I call to Kathy as she opens the door of her car, about to depart. She cups a hand to her ear to indicate that she is listening. "Why is my property so valuable? Anyone who buys it would tear down the house, I suppose, to build something as hideous as the things you sell. The island is inconvenient to get to and from. It's a poor choice for Hamptons dinner parties, unless one can accommodate a flotilla. It will take much longer to unload than your usual junk. So tell me, why do you want it? Really."

She stands still for a rare moment, then sighs deeply, as if she has just declared her undying love to a man she now discovers is stone-deaf.

"Harry March, you *are* an innocent," she says. "Location, location. Do you know what that means?"

"Neighborhood?" I answer feebly.

"No, poor boy. Not neighborhood. If location location simply meant 'neighborhood,' then any old jackass could tell a valuable house from a worthless one. It takes someone with vision to see what you've got here. Someone with a vision of himself as well as of everything else. Someone who recognizes his place in the universe. Someone lahk me. Someone lahk . . ."

"Don't say it!"

"You know what Ah think? Ah think Mr. Lapham will want to buy your island and flatten your house so that he may enjoy an unimpeded view of the beautiful surroundings to the west. That's what Ah think. He's quite the conservationist, you know." She steadies her gaze. "But he'll keep your dock, I'm pretty sure. He'll keep your dock."

"Why is that?" I ask.

"Because it's an *L*, Harry. From his viewpoint, a great big Lapham-size *L!*" She laughs and drives off.

I read somewhere that Charlie Chaplin once finished third in a Charlie Chaplin lookalike contest. I know exactly how he felt.

Seventeen

In the bellicose darkness of a summer evening, when the rain clouds inflate like black dirigibles, the wind cleaves the air like a cannonball shot from the deck of a battle-scarred frigate, the creek waves smack the beach like the rattle of a Gatling gun, and I have run out of martial imagery, I prepare for war. An hour from now, Lapham's workers will have departed the construction site, their day's mischief done, and I shall christen my Da Vinci at last.

"Finished your lecture yet?" Hector asks. His slim-reed hope is that, having neglected the Chautauqua presentation for most of the day, I will now get bogged down in it and forget my main project. How little he knows me. "Such a fascinating topic, the twentieth century," he tries. "So complex. So—how do you put it?—layered."

"I have my theme," I tell him, indicating Lapham's house with a flick of my head. "The details are easy." We are sitting side by side on the dock, listening to the ocean chug in its wash cycle.

It is a little after seven. I know that without having to look. And thanks to Kathy, the torsion spring lies in place, so I have nothing to do but wait. I've called the car to pick me up on Quogue Street at 8:45, in plenty of time to get me to La-Guardia for my flight, which I even remembered to confirm. I've packed. What have we here? A moment of calm? Hector starts to sing "When you come to the end of a perfect day," but I shut him up. He stares across at Lapham's with want and admiration. Yet he cannot help himself; he looks sweet.

"What?"

"Nothing."

This purple hour, how I reveled in it before the banging started. The almost-night wraps around everything like a complete and airtight thought, an image that works from all sides. And I don't mean just here on Noman, or here in Quogue. At the hour the sun gets ready to call it a day, even if thunderheads are about to break open at the seams, as they are right now, one can feel a lover's sigh cover the East End, something unheard for a million years since the Pleistocene glaciers bullied the landmass into shape, and the breakers crashed in on the rocks, rubbing and grinding, until they sculpted a shoreline.

Somewhere at this moment an antiques dealer is hauling

in the trestle tables and ladderback chairs from the front lawn of his shop on the highway where they have stood all day on siren display. Bathers (sun and ocean) make their slow processionals up the escarpments, their eyes stunned by the battle fatigue of a day at the beach. SUVs idle in front of the shops, while husbands pick up a last-minute lobster. Cigarette boats, their frantic engines tamed to a purring, slither through the locks of the Shinnecock Canal, and aim for their slips. Mothers in whites, with tennis rackets strapped to their backs like hunting bows, ride their bikes home. Kids, too. Even the estate sections breathe more evenly at this hour, as the sprinklers on timers spume and sputter all at once, and the residents, returned from whatever, adjust their showerheads, spray the salt from their skin, and do not talk. No sound on the fresh-washed streets but the clopping of a solitary jogger. The trophy children in their pj's read *Babar*.

Soon the villages will be left to the wheeling gulls and to the police cars crouching in the bushes, both poised for a late catch. Otherwise, it is a wholesale desertion of the out-of-doors, like the beginning of Gray's "Elegy." It leaves the world to darkness and to me. And to him.

"What?"

"Nothing."

In the purple hour, my father would recite that poem, Gray's "Elegy Written in a Country Churchyard." Formidable piece of work. Eighteenth century, of course. He could do it from memory, because that is how poetry was taught back then. One memorized Gray's "Elegy," which was incorporated into one's being, and thus became like an eye or a thumb; one had no choice but to feel improved by it.

Tonight he and my mother lie in the Quogue cemetery (not a churchyard; he never would have agreed to that), where small gray-and-white headstones convene in an eternally unadjourned town meeting. I once had hoped Chloe and I would lie there too, eventually, but I suppose the L.A. boneyards have more oomph. Great stone Gabriels spread their protective wings over the dust of moguls who denied Dalton Trumbo. Such a strange world.

Which reminds me: I ought to make out a will. I have tried to be careful with tonight's plan, but I still could wind up in the drink.

"Off to do more writing?" asks Hector. "Good idea. Take all the time you need."

Inside the house, I retrieve the camcorder that my children gave me for my last birthday. It was sort of a joke. They knew I'd long been of the opinion that the camcorder was responsible for the general lack of modesty abroad these days, that by enabling everyone to appear on television, it had contributed to the death of private life. They also suggested that I use it to record my own life as a warning to others. I've never even taken the thing out of its box before, but it seems simple enough to operate, and the kids had the forethought to include a tape. I return to the dock, set the camcorder on a piling, plug it in the outlet, and position myself before the lens, with the Da Vinci behind me. I am certain I look as comfortable as George Bernard Shaw or Arthur Conan Doyle in those primitive movie interviews in which, hands at their sides, they appear to be facing a firing squad. "This is my will and testament," I begin.

"Yahoo!" says Hector. He trots to my side. "I've always wanted you to make out a will. As your closest relative, I mean."

"Only geographically. If you want to stay while I'm taping, you'll have to be quiet."

"As a Doberman."

"To begin with . . ." I address the camcorder.

"Hallelujah!"

"I won't warn you again." He bows his head.

"To begin with, I wish to quote the poet Hesiod as an epigraph to this document. Hesiod, my kind of poet, wrote of the Ages of Man. As to his own times, he offered the following observation:

" 'Ah, if only I did not belong to the fifth age of men which is now come. Had I but died earlier, or come into the world later! For this is the iron age. These men are utterly corrupt. By day and by night they fret and the gods send them more and more gnawing cares. But they bring their greatest trouble upon themselves. Everywhere the right of might prevails, and city destroys its neighbor city. Whoever is true to his oath and is good and just finds no favor. Fairness and moderation are no longer esteemed. The wicked are allowed to harm the noble, to lie, and to swear false oaths. Nothing but misery is left to mortals, and no end of this mournful state is yet in sight.' "

"A bit flip for my taste," says Hector. "But I like it."

"And now to the more practical portions of the will: my bequests and requests." Hector sits up, his ears *way* up.

"To the people of the East End I leave my island, Noman, as a wildlife refuge. I would like to know that the children of the area, and especially the poorer ones, will have a place to study nature and generally enjoy themselves in a protected environment. Let there be many boats full of happy young ones going back and forth day and night across the creek in full view of the majestic house of the Laphams, who, I am sure, will delight in the round-the-clock squeals of excitement. I should warn you that there may be some opposition to this bequest from one Kathy Polite of Polite for the Elite, Realtors. But pay her no heed. She is known to be unbalanced, and it would be kinder simply to ignore her.

"To Chloe, Charles, Emma, and James I leave everything else I own, which admittedly is not much, except for what cash remains in the Money Room and a few book royalties that might provide an annuity sufficient for one good yearly family dinner in a two-star restaurant. Chloe, you are welcome to bring Joel to the dinner, at which you might raise a glass to my memory, but that is up to you. In any event, do not make a fuss about it and draw the silly attention of the other diners.

"To Dave's boy, Jack, I leave the cancellation of my loan. The money is his.

"To the British West Indies lady who takes ticket reservations for US Air I leave a round-trip two-day excursion to the Hamptons, to show her what she's been missing.

"To José the carpenter, who works on Dave's crew at Lapham's property, I leave a brand-new swimming pool, to be purchased from Miss Alvarez at Anthony's Aqua Heaven. Please see to it that the installation is as noisy as possible.

"To Miss Alvarez herself I wish to say, I am *not* a Romantic. But you may have my copy of *The Vanity of Human Wishes* anyway."

Hector goes into one of his bloodhound sniffing spasms to suggest his impatience.

"On the matter of my funeral: Joel, naturally, I leave this in your hands. But keep it simple. I know you may be tempted to go in another direction—a Gandhi-worthy procession of two or three million mourners stretching along the LIE, filling all the lanes, including the HOV, from the Moriches to Amagansett, all rending their garments and heaving with grief—but try to resist it.

"No eulogies, please. I do not want the congregants subjected to other writers talking about how much they meant to me.

"And I guess that's it," I tell the camcorder.

"Aren't you forgetting someone?" asks Hector.

"I don't think so. Whom did you have in mind?" I pretend to be perplexed about this. "Oh! You!" I love it that he can't help wagging his tail and betraying his excitement. I turn back to the camcorder.

"As to my dog, Hector, I leave him . . ."

"Yes? Yes?"

"I leave him to the Mexican carpenters across the creek. They are good guys and will take excellent care of him. Please tell them, however, that he is not to have nachos."

"But what about something for me? What will I inherit?"

"Try the earth."

I address the camcorder again. "One more thing. My epitaph? 'Do not resuscitate.'"

Eighteen

I've read that Mozart would grow melancholy when he approached the final stages of a composition, and that Velázquez would become surly and depressed when putting the final touches on a painting, and that Eugene O'Neill would so vigorously resist the moment when he was about to complete his final act that he would take long vacations in the tropics rather than endure the letdown of writing his last soggy lines. Such are my own emotions as I am about to survey my handiwork openly for what will be the first and possibly the last time.

I throw off the tarp with a flourish, the way a sculptor might remove the drape from a statue he is about to present to an audience in a gallery. The heavens cooperate in the moment. Thunder. Ka-boom! The Da Vinci is revealed in all its preposterous splendor. It is a work of art, of industrial art. The parts hug one another like the pieces of a gigantic Chinese puzzle box, functional and mysterious yet forbidding and smug in their completeness. I know how the builders of the Trojan Horse felt when they stood back from their masterwork and took it in, before the horse received a single Greek warrior. They had manufactured a weapon, to be sure, but first they had made a thing of beauty.

It is 7:41. Exactly ten minutes ago, at 7:31, Dave, Jack, and José and company packed up their gear and left Lapham's construction site. Exactly thirteen minutes ago, at 7:28, the site experienced its last bang of the day. I made a point of listening for it. I stood on my dock, craned my neck toward the creek, and waited. *Bang*. More than the last bang of the day, it was the last bang, period. *Bang*.

Now the storm arrives, not in a spray of droplets but with mature force. In the midst of the Sturm und Drang, I try to imagine how many white party tents are at this moment tottering on their tent poles on all the lawns of all the towns and villages of the East End. How many tent flaps are flapping; how many paper tablecloths are flying about in the wind; how many knives, forks, spoons, and napkins and plastic champagne flutes and tea lights are spinning through the air like shrapnel; how many canapés are sodden; how many contingency plans are hurriedly being put into effect; how many caterers are checking their contracts to verify that they cannot be held responsible for the weather; how many guests are apologizing for phoning at the last minute, unable to shake their summer colds; and how many hosts and hostesses are holding their heads with both hands as though they were in danger of flying off with the rest of the things.

The porch leaks and the storm strafes the house at a slant, entering the front door and pelting the remnants of the parlor wall into a viscous mound of plaster of Paris. The rain thickens and falls in metallic sheets, and I am soaked through and a bit chilled.

But the Da Vinci holds. The winches and the plates move easily. The pine ball I have been soaking in a tub of gasoline for the past two weeks lies in its pouch ready for ignition. Kathy Polite's braid performs brilliantly. I had misgivings, I must admit, but damn! She's as strong as a horse. I pull down the hurling arm using all the weight of my body. I fasten it at the base. I stand back. There. I take the extra-long fireplace matches I have been keeping dry, say a brief pagan prayer, and light the ball. It flares in the pouch like the sun itself, and for just a flash, the light it gives off illuminates everything in sight, including the looming skeleton of Lapham's house across the creek.

Outer walls, inner walls, pool-house walls, gazebo walls, atrium, aquarium, arboretum, auditorium, and asparagoretum walls; the piazza, esplanade, terrace, and gardens; the conservatory, the refectory, the aviary, apiary, chapel, stables, pantry, bomb shelter, French doors, pocket doors, the voissoir and the spandrel and the joists—all are lit up in the white of white heat, as if the scene were London bathed in floodlights during the Blitz.

Hector stares, then backs away. He is soaked through as well, his fur the color of unpolished silver, his mass diminished by the rain. Succinct little animal. He retreats to the shelter of the porch.

It's going to work, I know it. I did the research. I spent hours.

During World Wars I and II, soldiers tossed grenades using a type of torsion catapult. Aircraft carriers used catapult technology to launch planes from their decks. Years earlier, Samuel P. Langley, the Wright brothers' chief competitor, had built an aircraft called the Aerodrome that was propelled by a spring-powered catapult. And long before that, Alexander the Great had included catapults in his campaign artillery, substituting torsion springs for the gastaphetes, the old crossbow, in something like 400 B.C. By the third century B.C., great warriors were using the euthytonon for shooting arrows and the palintonon for throwing stone balls. And then later there were all of those flashy Romans and hairy Anglo-Saxons who fired off boulders, which I suppose constituted the world's first weapons of mass destruction. And what list would be complete without David, of happy memory, whose slingshot was a primitive form of catapult and whose opponent, like mine, had the advantage of size? Such is the brief history of this remarkable machine, which has served noble causes from the first ticks of time.

But none of the men who used the catapult in battle, not one of my distinguished and heroic blood brothers in arms, can have felt more satisfaction or a greater sense of purpose than do I at this moment.

Would that a tenor drum rolled. Would that a phalanx of French horns blared. Would that banners—swallowtails, fanions, and a couple of flammules—were flapping on pikes held aloft by Roman legionnaires wearing helmets and cuirasses and bearing shields and a glassus. Would that they might unfurl a tapestry depicting the anabasis of Cyrus the Younger as he marshaled his ten thousand Greek auxiliaries against Artaxerxes II. Would that a grandstand were packed with the great people of history—Dr. Johnson, Shakespeare, Dante, Beethoven, Vermeer, Newton, Curie, Gandhi, Michelangelo, King, Dearie, Gilliam, and of course, da Vinci—all on their feet cheering.

They acknowledge me. I acknowledge them. In my bearing I try to strike a balance between the demeanor of a victorious general immensely honored and that of a foot soldier simply doing his duty. Now all is hushed. A lone snare drum thrums a solemn march, and I am carried back to the earliest bright moments of the American Revolution, when all was bugles, fife, and promise, and the first Laphams were lost, or confused, at sea.

I step forward. The rain grows sleety. I pull the trigger device. The arm is released from the slip hook, and the pine ball shoots forward at a forty-five-degree angle, just as Sir Ralph promised it would. The fireball is launched at so high a trajectory that it competes with the storm for command of the night. It trails a bluish light into the black rain, and makes a deep *whoosh*, like a wind in the Arctic, audible even in the midst of the thunder and the massive torrent. Hector hunkers down and tucks his head between his paws. The rain crashes, the air sizzles with lightning. A clap of thunder I hear as applause.

Mouth open, eyes fixed, I await the hit, listen for the crash, watch for the moment of impact when the House of Lapham will flare into its own crematorium. A gasp. A blink. I follow the flight of the ball as a parent might gaze upon a child heading off to make his fortune in the world, and my heart thrills with sadness and pride and expectation.

And then I hear something terrible yet familiar. And then I see something even more terrible. The fireball that was growing smaller and smaller in its flight away from me—a medicine ball diminishing to a bowling ball to a golf ball—all of a sudden appears to have reversed its evolution, as if in a parallax, and now seems (am I imagining this?) a bit bigger, and a bit bigger. Definitely bigger.

What happens next I cannot bear to relate. Thus I shall describe the event as I imagine *The Southampton Press* will describe it a week hence, in a piece squeezed between one on the soaring prices of summer rentals and another announcing a fund-raiser for Hillary Clinton at the home of P. Diddy. *The Southampton Press* is a responsible paper, so, to my regret, it will get the story right.

A large house under construction was nearly destroyed when a fiery ball headed straight for it was diverted at the last second. Witnesses who happened to catch sight of the projectile as it flew its course in a heavy rainstorm reported that it looked like a small meteor or a new type of bomb. Police are certain it was the work of either teenage pranksters or Al Qaeda. As a result of the incident, the Office of Homeland Security has put all the Hamptons, including Quogue, on orange alert.

Fortunately the construction site, which is the eight-acre future home of the Laphams of Newport, R.I., Darien, Ct., Hobe Sound, Fla. and several other residences in America and Europe, was saved from total destruction by the activation of a state-of-the-art air conditioner belonging to Mr. Lapham, sold under the brand name Tilles Blowhard. When the thermostat on the Blowhard sensed the presence of extreme heat in the atmosphere around Mr. Lapham's house, the fireball having raised the air temperature to something higher than the desired 65 degrees Fahrenheit, a blower of exceptional power blasted a cold wind at the projectile and blew it straight back in the direction from which it had come. Witnesses far removed from the blast in East Moriches, Center Moriches, and beyond reported that the noise sounded like the word *awe*.

Unfortunately, the fireball then landed on a small, undistinguished house on an island in the creek bordering the Lapham property, occupied by reclusive writer Harry March, and burned it to the ground . . .

. . . though not before I rush in to grab Hector, *The Vanity of Human Wishes*, my Blossom Dearie CDs, my Junior Gilliam photo, and, I don't know why, my pen and a writing pad. I guess I won't need US Air or the hired car, after all. Rude of me not to call and cancel, but the phone is melting.

The newspaper article ought also to mention that not only is my house on fire; my entire island, a victim of the "driest summer in memory," is likewise ablaze. Tennessee in flames. My house is gone; my island is going. The fire spreads over it in scattered orange triangles, both equilateral and isosceles. I sit on my beach with my feet in the water and stare at the last two things to go, the Da Vinci and my wooden rowboat. The boat flares up nicely. I have no way out but to swim, and in this storm, and with my injured toe, I may not make it.

In the house, only one structure remains unaffected by the fire: the statue of Chloe sits absorbed in the news, forever and ever, indestructible and immortal, God bless her. The Hungarian dwarf would be pleased. My dock holds as well, probably because it too has its feet in the water.

Hector issues a volley of machine-gun barks at the flames. He is especially helpful in emergencies. I carry him over to *Sharon*, place him in her hull, and guide him toward Lapham's shore. He looks annoyed, insofar as he can look anything, and tosses me a sarcastic bark.

"Satisfied?" he asks.

"I'm trying to save your life."

"The good Lord will save my life," he says. I wish the remote had a torpedo button. As he fades from my sight I hear the loud, atonal strains of the Navy hymn.

An empty bottle of Absolut vodka floats up to me, and I begin to scribble a letter to put inside in hopes that the vessel will ride the waterways north and eventually reach the Chautauquans. Since it is a vodka bottle, it stands a better than even chance.

To the good people of Chautauqua:

I'm sorry I will not be able to be with you for your program on the twentieth century. But I'm dead. I would like to take this postmortem opportunity, nonetheless, to tell you about the lecture I cannot deliver in person.

Are you ready to hear this, Chautauqans? Are you sitting down? Yes, of course. You're always sitting down.

A loud pop from a burning log startles me, and I turn to see the fire gobbling up my cord of wood, then rushing to the hill as if in a panic, and spreading everywhere. This is not the best atmosphere for writing. But it does add a certain urgency, a real deadline. I continue:

My lecture was to be about Lapham, my sordidly ambitious, absurdly self-important, earsplittingly noise-making, unwanted neighbor Lapham. For anything you want to know about the destructive, witless twentieth century, you may look to Lapham. Every time you see a monument to personal glory, some dumbass splurge at the expense of taste and good works—some house, for example, that is thirty times larger than it needs to be—there's your twentieth century for you, and your twenty-first to boot.

So just say it: Lapham. Scream it: Lapham. Wear a button: Down with Lapham. Paste a bumper sticker to your fender: No Laphams on Board.

Now the air is clogged with smoke. I try to fan myself with the writing pad, but it doesn't work. I'm going to get this done regardless.

The foregoing, in a nutshell, was to be my lecture—a plaint-cum-fire-and-brimstone oration, a call to arms against my neighbor and his ilk, who with their banging and their flabby dreams have taken away my world, the world I wanted to hang on to.

And what was this world I wanted to hang on to? Why, dear Chautauquans, it was *you*, your world of thought and of art and of friendship and of usefulness to others. Perhaps that last above all: usefulness to others. For no other reason would I have come to you to speak. And when your invitation arrived on the very day that Lapham began to build his house, I knew then that I would have something to tell you, especially you who, in your slightly pixilated but fundamentally lovely way, hold fast to the same world that my parents and their parents before them tried to preserve within the little land of the Marches down through time.

But here comes the sad part of my lecture. For I had hoped to inform you that against all odds, I had defeated Lapham, reversed his upward direction, or at the very least slowed him down. Indeed, my original intention was to relate to you a tale of conquest, and to suggest how each of you might make that tale your own. Yet to my sorrow and embarrassment, I must report not my own victory but rather his. The fact that I am dead speaks for itself. And the object lesson I have learned, after all the high-flown theorizing and the gathering of evidence, and all the clever conclusions that the mind is capable of, is that the Age of Lapham—in all its vapidity and self-regard, in all its empire building and vanity, in its mindless dollars and its most powerful air conditioner in the world—wins. Just that: it wins.

As if to support my conclusion, the heat from the fire has grown ovenlike. Where is the Blowhard when you need it? More popping of logs. When I turn around this time, all I see behind me is a sky in flames. Perhaps this is more atmosphere than I needed. Only a few sentences to go.

So what lesson may I bring you, my worthy Chautauquans, as I picture this letter of mine being read to you, seventy-five hundred strong, sitting in your amphitheater—

and read to you, what's more, by two teenage interns who came across the vodka bottle as they were making out on your beach? The lesson is this: the reason Lapham has won this time, and will win again, and will always win, is that *you* allow it to happen. You sit together in your amphitheater, but you do not stand together.

Rise up, Chautauquans. (I stand for dramatic emphasis.) Rise up to defend your world of thought and poetry and music and your lacy red-and-blue porches stuffed with gladiolas and your leafy glades and your true-blue lakes. Rise as Lapham is rising, and smite him not with weapons—they will backfire, take it from me—but rather with your books and your songs and your laughter. Beat him back with your modesty, the knowledge of your frailty—that is to say, with your humanity.

Or if you prefer, you all can go out and live on your separate islands and seethe and fume and rant and go nuts in the company of your sarcastic, barking Bible-thumping dog. It worked for *me*.

Nineteen

Sirens whine in the dark distance. I sit soaking my feet in the tide, my toes, including the bad one, rummaging through the pebbles in the creek bed. All around, the reek of scorched wood mixes with the weedy smell of decay. The greedy fire feeds on everything, insistent against the rain. The megaphone lies on its side nearby, next to *The Vanity of Human Wishes*. I am too far gone to interpret this symbolically.

Across the creek, red lights flash and spin. I can just make out the dim shapes of the rescue vehicles: a fire truck, an ambulance, many police cars. Other cars pull up, including—my heart sinks—a creamy Mercedes. I hear the unmistakable banjo music of the Old South.

"Harry March! You swindler! You crook!" She is using the bullhorn this time. "We had a bargain!"

Police and firemen are yelling to me as well. It seems that

they have brought along every available vehicle for my rescue except the floating kind, and now, with the flames at my back creeping toward me, they are trying to decide how to get me off my island. A strange yet satisfying peace comes over me. I may die after all, but Kathy Polite will wind up with a derelict property, an eyesore. And Lapham too. I will have accomplished the unthinkable: I will have dragged Hamptons real estate values downward.

"Answer me, Harry. Are you there? Are you still alive?" She cares.

"Yes, Magnolia." I aim my megaphone into the pulverizing rain. "I live, but not for long. And yet I die content because my diabolical plan worked. It worked! I tricked you out of your beautiful braid of hair so that I could use it in my Da Vinci catapult, which I designed intentionally to boomerang and set fire to my unspoiled island and cheat you out of your fortune. What do you think of that?"

"Crazy as a loon," she shouts. "Ah'm arranging to rescue you so that Ah can kill you mahself."

"Stay away." Give me death rather than another conversation with that woman. Hell, I know I'll probably swim and live, but I am determined to sit here till the last possible minute. I don't want to rush it. On the other side of the creek, I will have to talk to people, answer questions, become an object of sympathy. Someone will offer me a Dixie cup of brandy and a towel, and wrap me in a red plaid blanket. Strangers may hug me. Kathy may hug me. Gaah. One tiny bright thought: given that I alone have suffered the consequences of my actions, the police most likely will not arrest me, unless attempted catapult is a felony.

But if I am to be true to eighteenth-century principles, I should take whatever they dish out to me like a man-sized man. I should concede defeat, lick my wounds, and pick up and settle elsewhere. Miss Alvarez had a point about my behaving like a Romantic. The Da Vinci debacle certainly was a Romantic's act. In my single-mindedness, I may have lost sight of the more generous purposes of a simple way of life. Could be. Somewhere, I am sure, a calm, quiet place awaits me where I may do something worthwhile again. Another island, perhaps. Or a little cottage near the sea, far removed from developers, removed from Lapham. And, there is always Vermont. For everyone, in every time of despairing optimism, there is always Vermont.

If I have lost my possessions, I still have essential intangibles: Chloe's cautious but genuine affection, the love of my children, and the devotion of Hector, I am fairly certain, wherever he may be. And they have mine. As for romance, I might wait for Miss Alvarez, if she would wait for me. When I turn seventy, she'll be thirty, hardly any difference in our ages at all. Then too, she is so serious-minded that by the time she's forty she'll look older than I do. I think I'll mention this to her as a selling point when I propose.

Who knows? Maybe I will begin to write again, practice what I preached to the Chautauquans, and use the weapons I believe in. Why not? I could write the story of all this—of me and Hector and Lapham and the Da Vinci—and pass it off as a novel. It's a pretty good story. Not that anyone would believe it.

Behind me and to the sides, the fire sparks and flares, but the wind is no longer against me, so its approach has slowed, at least for the moment. The flames make a huge jack-o'-lantern of the house. The shingles crackle and sputter. The creek is black, and across on Lapham's side the headlights of the rescue vehicles beam like twenty pairs of surprised eyes. I stare back, just as surprised. Another pair of eyes joins the automotive party. The latest arrival whispers like a Rolls. Suddenly my toe acts up and smiles more broadly.

"Harry! Mr. Lapham is here!" Kathy calls to me. "He drove over from his very-nice-Ah-must-say rental cottage in Southampton when he heard about the fireball. He was so pleased that the Blowhard worked. Do not despair!"

I peer into the shadows on the far side of the water to try to see what Lapham looks like. It is too dark, though I sense a great deal of hurried activity, which makes me nervous.

"Mr. March! Mr. March!" A high-pitched voice cuts

through the rain and the wind. "Sir!" It identifies itself as be-longing to the faithful mouthpiece, Damenial Krento. "Sir! Mr. Lapham is coming for you himself!"

"What do you mean?" I shout back, with all the insincerity that question implies.

"Mr. Lapham has heard of your plight. He is coming for you in his Hinckley Picnic Boat."

"No!" I yell.

"Do not worry, sir. The Hinckley Picnic Boat is the best powerboat in the world! It draws just six inches of water. It has both gas and jet engines, you know, and costs four hun-dred and fifty thousand dollars."

"I don't care about the Hinckley Picnic Boat. Tell Lapham to stay put!"

This can't be happening. Life, so called, cannot be so cruel as this. After months of steaming and cursing him out, after all the planning and plotting, after a lifetime of resisting Lapham and all the other Laphams stretching back to the dawn of their dismal lineage—after the banging—am I now to be reduced to a state of impotency in which Lapham must be responsible for saving my skin?

I'd rather roll into the creek. I'd rather swallow mouthfuls of sand until I asphyxiate myself. To be in his debt would be bad enough, but to owe him my life! To have to say, Thanks, Lapham, old boy, and then engage in the other pleasantries to follow: Why yes! I'd love to play eighteen holes at Stinkerton. Why yes! I'd love to come to dinner. Why yes! I'd love to sit in your two-thousand-square-foot dining alcove, under the crystal chandelier imported from Berlin and left over from Kristallnacht, and play a game of whist, and afterward watch a movie in your home theater that seats six hundred. It's just like the old Palace! Why yes! *Field of Dreams,* it's my favorite too! Why yes! I'd love some asparagus stalks. But how to grasp them?

"Go away!" I shout into the darkness. "I'm fine."

"You're *not* fine. You're a mess." A different voice. That of Miss Alvarez. "Idiot!" she shouts. "Take the help."

"You go away too," I shout, not entirely unhappy that she is here.

"Do you want to die out there?" Kathy sounds frighteningly tender. I slide more of my body into the water to cool off.

"Señor March! You must do as we say!" The Mexicans too have driven over for the occasion. More shouting still. A raucous fugue from various sources. I picture the Shinnecock Indians, who are wondering if they will ever get their casino and thus achieve the wealth and contentment of the Pequots in Connecticut; the members of the 1938 Hurricane Society, who are wondering if they will ever get rid of the Indians and their loathsome tepee on the highway; Dr. Whatshisname, who is wondering if his genius will be acknowledged during his lifetime; Parrot Light, the reporter, who is wondering whether she should describe the fire as a "blaze" or a "conflagration"; the Amherst English major, who is wondering if he should change his thesis title to "Death Comes to a Minor Talent"; the two teenage Kristens from Westhampton, who are wondering nothing whatsoever; the Panelle Hall panel people, who are just now making plans for a panel to be entitled "Fire: How Safe Are We?"; One More Time's proprietor; the policewoman; Mr. and Mrs. Turtle; the doctor; the cabdriver; Medusa and Fairy Tale Dora, who is calling to me in Spanish; Mrs. Damato, the librarian who is dolefully shaking her head; and Dave and his boy, Jack, who at first wonders if all this would make a good film, then tastefully decides against it. My entire social circle, present at the destruction. Everyone except the US Air lady, who is undoubtedly too dutiful to leave her post, and the FedEx man, who very likely is celebrating privately.

"It's a matter of principle," I shout, louder than ever. "If I put my life in Lapham's hands, I capitulate. I give in to everything I despise. I surrender to all that is bringing down civilization. I—"

"Put a sock in it," she shouts. I cannot tell whether the voice belongs to Kathy or Miss Alvarez. I sit, knees up in the self-protective fetal position, and I clutch *The Vanity of Human Wishes* to my chest.

Hmmm hmmm hmmm: I hear the whir of Lapham's mini-yacht coming toward me. He zeroes in using searchlights that flood the creek with long and probing beams, like the ones with which guards at Sing Sing might comb the prison yard for an escaping convict. Mentally I measure the beams, which sparkle in the rain and seem not merely to search but to pry, to investigate every chink and crevice in the surroundings, even digging beneath the agglutinate banks of the shore.

On he comes. The ravenous bow of the Hinckley Picnic Boat rises and falls as the vessel throws off bulbous wakes on both sides, tidal waves in the making. The bow trails a blue-green phosphorescence that melts into the night. All I am able to do is stare. I don't suppose a boat like that could hit a rock and sink.

I rise and limp to the dock at the extreme end of the *L* to get a better view of him. Amid the slapping of waves against the Hinckley's hull, I hear a familiar sound: Hector barking. He has Hector! Now I'm sorry I saved him. "Traitor!" I yell. He merely barks back.

The wind howls like a wolf. The rain drops like a theater curtain. Out in the boat, something is moving. I see it: a sleeve, a hand. He is waving at me. Lapham, in full-blown brainless bonhomie, is waving at me.

Bang bang bang bang bang. His boat bangs against the water. Always a bang with Lapham. He carries the noise of hell with him. And he is clearer now, nearer.

Dear God: Do something. Even if I don't believe in You, why be petty?

Dear Satan: Is it too late for us to make a deal? Or did that one with Kathy count?

The whirring ceases. The banging ceases. The engine has stopped. Hector has stopped. Now the wind and the rain have stopped as well. Just like that, stopped. Deciding to keep the Hinckley Picnic Boat at a safe remove from the fire, Lapham drops anchor, hooks a small ladder to the gunwale, and climbs down into the water, which I assume is no more than six inches deep. He appears to be wearing a blue blazer and a commodore's cap tilted back on his head like a cocky Air Force ace. He slogs and splashes, his shadow rising against the sky, rising and rising and striding in its terrible confidence toward me. He is waving more frantically now, giddily, still in silhouette.

Now he pauses to get his bearings. He cannot be thirty feet away. And all at once the moonlight breaks through the clouds and begins to draw a path, first upon the creek, then upon the beach, and now upon Lapham, who is revealed to me at last. I gaze in stupefaction from the end of my dock, where to my right the Da Vinci smolders.

He is six feet tall and of heavy build, I think. He may be slimmer or thicker, it's hard for me to be sure. And if you told me he was really six-foot-four or five-foot-eight, I could not contradict you, because he carries himself like a thug with a swagger, and yet also like a dandy with a little skip.

His face: the moon illuminates it so gradually, so ceremonially, that I have ample opportunity to take note of its features from top to bottom. Yet I can tell you only that it unveils itself as a face that resists, indeed argues against, description.

The strands of hair that show beneath the peak of his cap are blond, perhaps gray or dirty blond, or auburn, or brown, possibly black. The hairline is neither rounded nor a widow's peak, neither receding nor encroaching on the eyes. The forehead seems neither broad nor narrow, neither high nor low. There are wrinkles in the expanse over the eyebrows, and yet there aren't. No sooner do I spot one wrinkle than it is gone, and then, when gone, it reappears. I see age in the face, and then I do not. The eyebrows themselves are both bushy and sparse, extended and abbreviated. I do not mean that one brow is one thing and the other another, but rather that each appears to possess all of these qualities at once. So too do the eyes themselves, the so-called windows of the soul, which in this case are both blue and brown. No, green. No, olive. No, hazel. No, gray. A sort of grayish, hazelish, bluish, oliveish, brownish-green. Yes, that's it. And the cheekbones, they are both high and sunken. And the ears, they protrude like the handles of teacups, yet they are barely visible, stuck flat against the sides of the head. There are lobes. There are not.

The nose is Roman and aquiline, but with a crooked ridge and a square knob at the tip, which also—I know this will sound odd—appears raddled, like W. C. Fields's nose, but at the same time elongated and of anteater grandeur, like Louis Calhern's. And yet it is snubby too, like Condoleezza Rice's. He has Betty Boop's mouth, but then again his mouth is larger than Betty's, and the lips look like two thumbs pressed against each other, or maybe like two crayons, Crayolas, and yet different. And the chin, it is prominent and recessive, jutting and retreating. I'm sorry. I know this all is terribly imprecise, but it is the best I can do. Perhaps I'm too exhausted to be accurate. Perhaps it's the night, or the light.

In any case, as he steps toward me, I find myself reacting to his arrival in the strangest way. Against my will, against my history and my family's history, and certainly against all that has transpired on this day, I feel a counterforce arising in me, a shock of gratitude, a chill of recognition, a sort of— what?—epiphany of fellow feeling. For all that he is and represents, Lapham has come to save me, after all. If he is encumbering this drowning man with help, he does not mean to do it. He only means well. However awkward he is, however preposterous in that blazer (Jesus! It's double-breasted!) and that cap (commodore of what?), in his own mind, such as it is, he only means well.

I sense myself sliding into feelings of warmth toward him, much as I imagine I might harbor affection for some large, dumb animal, a yak or an ox, if it trampled me in a field and then, driven by some instinctive chromosome of kindness, returned to sniff me and nuzzle my shoulder. And so I am aware that involuntarily I am nuzzling back, and whereas the act itself may be alien to me, the spirit it evokes is nevertheless familiar, though it is one I have not experienced in a long time, in ten months at least, that's for sure. Humane: I am feeling humane.

Steadily, relentlessly, he splashes in my direction. His pillarlike legs, covered in white linen, part the waters. His feet, covered by low-cut tennis shoes, cast a spray as he hits the shore. My hand begins to lift on its own, as if performing in a séance. I am rising (dare I say it?) toward a friendly wave. My throat clears. I am rising (can this be happening?) toward a "Hi!" Timid and faint though it may be, there is no denying its approach. I am nearly there, at both the wave and the "Hi!"

But he walks past me. Lapham walks past me. He does not see me. I am here, plain as the moon can make me, about to welcome him to my island and my bosom. But he strides straight past what's left of the Da Vinci, what's left of the dock, and me, until he has proceeded ten yards or so inland, as far as he can go toward the fire. There he halts. Save for this one open patch, the island still burns like a long, thin log, every inch of it in flame and embers.

I turn and watch him, his back to me now, as he stuffs his hands into his pockets and relaxes his shoulders. He looks to the left. He looks to the right. He breathes in. He breathes out. At last he speaks. And his voice is not flaccid, as I have guessed it will be. It sounds like a gargle laced with a wheeze. And it booms.

"What a venue!" he says. "What a venue!"

I tear off my clothes and toss them in a heap. I perch, I crouch, I spring into a stupendous belly flop, and then I swim into the night, away from him, away from here. Suddenly, behind me, I hear another splash. Hector has leapt from the Hinckley Picnic Boat. He catches up and paddles beside me. His head glows silver in moonlight. We do not say a word.